Tobermory Days

Tobermory Days
stories • from • an • island

Lorn Macintyre

Argyll
publishing

First published in 2003 by
Argyll Publishing
Glendaruel
Argyll PA22 3AE
Scotland
www.skoobe.biz

The author has asserted his moral rights.

British Library Cataloguing-in-Publication Data.
A catalogue record for this book is available from
the British Library.

ISBN 1 902831 56 X

Scottish
Arts Council

The publisher acknowledges subsidy from the Scottish Arts
Council towards the publication of this volume.

For permission to quote on page 184 from Sorley MacLean's
'Elegy for Calum I MacLean', grateful thanks to Carcanet Press.

Cover photo: stockscotland.com

Origination: Cordfall Ltd, Glasgow

Printing: Mackays of Chatham Ltd

To Angus and Betty
irrepressible parents

ACKNOWLEDGEMENTS

The Curam was previously published in *Flamingo Book of New Scottish Writing* (HarperCollins 1997).

The story *Saskatchewan* first appeared in *Flamingo Book of New Scottish Writing* (HarperCollins 1998).

Saskatchewan was also published in *Stories from Scotland* (Macmillan, 2001).

Housebound/Peaches appeared in *Shorts: the Macallan/ Scotland on Sunday short story collection* (Polygon, 2002).

Contents

1.
Candid Camera

After her husband's death Alice Maclean laid out some of his possessions on their bed and invited their grown-up children to choose a memento. Murdo took the classic Parker, part of the flight of three with the golden arrows that the bank manager had worn above his heart. Archie Maclean had loved the feel of a good fountain pen, writing his signature with a flourish on official documents, or jotting down lines of verse on the back of an envelope to recite at one of his famous ceilidhs.

Calum, the other son, took the black-faced wrist watch with the white numerals that his father had bought from a flying boat pilot who was subsequently lost while shadowing a convoy arriving from Nova Scotia. Eilidh, their sister, chose his wallet.

'What would you like, dear?' Alice asked her other daughter.

Marsaili was looking at the masculine property laid out on the quilt. She could have taken the framed scroll of the freedom of the burgh conferred on her father, with the signatures of the Provost and Town Clerk beside the elaborate red seal. Instead she went down on her knees and pulled a small shabby suitcase from under the bed.

'You're not taking these?' Alice said, aghast. 'I was going to throw them out.'

'If you had, you would have thrown away part of the history of this island,' her daughter warned her as she sprung the corroded catches with her thumbs. The case was full of small grey spools, one side yellow. Marsaili picked one up and held it to the window. Her father had written on it with one of his precious pens: 'Snow, Main Street, 1960.'

The cine camera came into Archie Maclean's hands by default. One of his customers, Jimmy Laing, had been buying it on hire purchase from a place in England, but had fallen off a ladder while painting the Treasure Trove for the tourist season, and couldn't meet the instalments. The bank manager took them over with the camera, plus a payment of twenty pounds to Jimmy, who was very happy with the transaction.

The camera was silver coloured, in the shape of a cumbersome pistol, with a recessed key in the side for winding the mechanism. At the lens was a lever for adjusting the zoom. Bessie in the chemist's ordered the films for the banker, and when he had shot them he sealed them in a yellow envelope which he addressed to a place in the south. A week or so later, the processed film came back. The sitting-room was converted for the showing. Marsaili lifted the lithograph of a stag from the wall, while her father set up the projector on a table, using a Gaelic book to prop it up at the correct height. A rectangular dazzle hits the wall. The film running through the sprockets makes a sniggering sound, and then the image tilts, as if Archie had slipped with the camera. It takes ten seconds for the picture to steady, but the shimmering effect isn't out of focus. It's snow falling on Main Street, a rare occurrence beside the sea.

Pan now to the Co-operative, where Mrs Bean MacDougall emerges with her shopping. The cameraman lingers on the hefty legs encased in fur boots. When she falls on her backside, potatoes tumbling over the pavement, they are tracked by the sure camera. The audience in the sitting-room of the bank house is helpless with laughter, but Alice rebukes her family. 'It's not funny. Why did you film it, Archie?' she challenges her husband, as if he were responsible for Mrs Bean MacDougall's fall.

No subject was too lowly for the banker's camera as he stood in the little tower off the sitting-room above Main Street, like a look-out high on a ship. In so many of the films the background is the granite obelisk of the clock, with stone seats round the base. It was presented to the town in memory of Miss Amelia Horseman, an intrepid Englishwoman who had walked the rim of an active South Seas volcano in smouldering shoes before settling in this Hebridean town where she did Christian work, sometimes lecturing in native costume. The luminous face of the clock has been a beacon used by boats entering the bay in darkness for a hundred years.

The clock was in the centre of the four hundred yard curve that comprised Main Street. Up to Victorian times there was no barrier between the street and the bay, but when a drunk fell head-first into the sea in an exceptionally high spring tide in 1903, railings were installed, and painted white every third year.

The town had been established in the late eighteenth century as a fishing station, but the shoals of herring had failed to materialise in the sound outside the bay. Instead it became a safe anchorage. At the north end was the new pier, built at the turn of the century to accommodate the increasing number of pleasure steamers. Halfway along Main Street beside the memorial clock was the old pier, made from big blocks of stone without mortar. Though it had steps at the end, it was an awkward place for boats to discharge passengers or cargo.

Archie has often stood on the old pier on a summer evening

and panned along Main Street – soft focus shots, because the light can be exceptional here, tinted by a blue haze. His pan begins at the new pier, passing the petrol station run by Tommy Hepburn, an incomer who lost a leg at Jutland; the rare post box erected for King Edward VIII; the block of tall tenements, built by speculators in the early nineteenth century, beginning with the brightly painted Ceilidh Hotel and Bar, blue some years, yellow for others; more tenements; the paper shop; the gap for the brae up to the top of the town; what used to be Murchison's Store but is now a fish shop; tenements again; the Treasure Trove, which sells souvenirs to the tourists, silver Iona crosses especially popular; the bank with the house above which Archie's lens lingers on, because it is his home and the most impressive building on Main Street, apart from the churches. Scottish baronial with crowstepped gables and a tower, the bank is more a small castle than a commercial building.

The camera continues its sweep: Joey the butcher; the shop that used to be called the Island Emporium; the Co-operative, the post office, formerly the Custom House. Johnson and Boswell were blown into the bay during their Hebridean tour and stayed in the Custom House, then an inn. After a supper of fowls and green vegetables, the good Doctor sat discoursing with the natives on the idea of virtue. He took their nods as assent, but they couldn't understand him because they didn't have a word of English.

Boswell recorded in his *Journal*: 'We were served supper by a most comely wench showing a great deal of leg. By the use of signs I was able to make her understand that I wished to see her later. By the light of a magnificent moon over the bay I enjoyed her against the back door of the inn, until the banging of her buttocks brought out the innkeeper, who thought it was a late traveller looking for sustenance and a bed.'

Beyond the former Custom House is the Free Church, a large building with a notable stained glass window in the shape of a wheel. Where once a packed congregation took up the doleful psalms sung by the precentor, machines now clatter, making Celtic-patterned sweaters for the tourists.

The Royal Yacht entered this bay on a late summer evening in 1847, but because of the downpour Queen Victoria didn't come ashore. However, she wrote in her *Journal* that the town was 'prettily situated' and 'brightly illuminated for our visit'.

Archie Maclean's camera continues its track. More tenements, more shops, until, at the other end of the bay, the distillery. Many locals still remember the heady breeze from its chimney in its heyday and the barrels being trundled down the slipway. Because of the free drams, the workers never went home sober, and there were many cases of cirrhosis.

Beside the distillery, the stone shed that housed the black-smith's, in the days when the only traffic on the island was horses and carts. The MacNaughtons had run it for generations, the rumps of horses half-way inside the building as the smith hammered the glowing shoe into shape on the anvil, the strikes punctuating his expressive Gaelic. Next to the defunct blacksmith's with its rusted anvil, like the horn of some prehistoric creature, is MacDowell's Garage with its antiquated petrol pump.

The Arms is a hundred yards from the distillery, and the bank manager is now in the tower of his house with his cine camera, waiting for worthies to emerge from that hostelry. He tracks Sandy Anderson groping his way home along the wall, as if he has lost his sight through bad whisky. He catches Murdo the tall lean tinker, with his diminutive wife in tow, stopping visitors at the clock to give them misleading information on the town's history in exchange for money for drink.

Archie amassed his archive in the brown leather case under his bed, writing the date and the principal event on the small reels. He knew what he was doing. The characters were dying, and he wanted to record their quaint walks before they went. He also turned his camera out over the bay, to film yachts arriving. The white helm of the *Sea Wolf* – said to have been Goering's yacht – slides into view, but because the camera had no sound the anchor chain slithers silently under the calm water. Another boat, another memory. A lone piper standing in a stern at the Regatta, playing a silent reel to the town. Footage of waves crashing over the white railings, drenching Black's shop. In one film, Archie caught a couple copulating in the stern of a yawl one breathless evening. It was only a fleeting shot, but enough to make him stop the projector because most of the audience were under-age.

Marsaili took this precious archive to her Glasgow home, and long after her father was gone she would project a film on the dining-room wall, and be back on the island. The trouble was, for modesty as well as technical reasons, Archie Maclean had never turned the camera on himself, so he has not even one walk-on part in his own productions. The nearest he came was his ghostly reflection in the curved glass of the tower room window as he filmed another local worthy taking the entire width of Main Street on his way home from the pub.

However, on her sideboard Marsaili has a striking picture of her father. It was taken against the backdrop of the bay at Regatta time. It shows a well-built, benign-looking man, a former Highland Games athlete whose records still endure. He wears horn-rimmed glasses, and his silver hair is combed back from his high forehead. His moustache is trimmed, and the pens are arrayed in the pocket above his heart.

Sometimes Archie took his cine camera to the mainland, manhandling it under his coat as if he had come to rob a rival bank with a lethal weapon. The banker hated to spend even one night away from his beloved island, so footage of the mainland is very rare in his collection. However, a pipe band is silently blowing and beating on the pier, with the steamer, the *Lochspelvie,* behind. This was the boat that served the island for over fifty years, a daily service that only the most ferocious storm could prevent sailing.

Neither Archie nor his wife Alice was native. They had both been born and raised in the mainland town that was the port for the island. But two generations back Archie's people, a family of stonemasons, had left the island to look for work, and had helped to build, above the town, the hydropathic which had gone bankrupt before completion, and whose stones had been pillaged to build the surrounding villas. Alice, whose family had been domestic servants before acquiring a boarding house on the seafront, worked in Miss Munro's Dress Shop.

Archie, the accountant in the bank in John Street, was informed that he was being transferred to the island as bank manager. He was delighted, because though he was a native Gaelic speaker, the language was dying out in the town, and on the island he would get the chance to improve his grasp of it.

Alice wasn't keen to go and live there. She liked the town she had grown up in. However, her husband had always wanted to be a manager, so she packed her china in tea chests and got a reliable firm to handle the shipment of the furniture.

On her first crossing on the *Lochspelvie* the container was sitting on the deck, and her children, the two girls and two boys, were sitting with her up on the slatted seat that could be turned into a life-raft. It was a beautiful summer day, and she pointed out the imposing castle on the rock, and the mountains. The island seemed a romantic place to be going to.

Where was her husband on this first voyage? Down in the bar, talking in Gaelic with some of the travellers, 'finding out about the island,' as he told his wife, when he came on deck to join his family. The steamer was turning out of the sound, and there was the island's town in front of them.

'That's our house,' Archie pointed out the baronial building to his children.

Marsaili, her sister and two brothers fought over which of the five bedrooms they were each to have in the spacious bank house.

Eventually, with her father's support, Marsaili won the right to inhabit the tower room above the sitting-room, but on condition that she would vacate it and sleep in the downstairs study when people came to stay.

The furniture was carried up the impressive wrought-iron staircase, the mahogany sideboard into the dining-room, the sofa and two arm-chairs into the sitting-room. The pepper-and-salt cat, which had been brought across in a basket, stayed in its new home for one night, then defected next door to the Treasure Trove. For the rest of its long life it slept among the souvenirs in the window.

By nine o' clock that first night the matrimonial bed had been bolted together and most of the furniture had found a place. Alice had made her exhausted family tea and sandwiches, which they were consuming in the sitting-room when the doorbell rang. They heard the storm-door opening, and then slow feet on the stairs. The man who stood in the doorway was short and stout. He was wearing a grey raincoat, and a grey soft hat with a snappy brim. A stick was hooked over his arm, and there was a dog at his heels. Marsaili would later say that he looked as if he had a pistol in his pocket.

'I'm John MacDougall, come to welcome you to the island.'

The stranger was invited into the sitting-room, but declined tea. Marsaili would watch this man's habits over the years and sometimes mock them to her amused family. He would hook one foot over his stick, which lay along his leg against the sofa where he always sat. When he smoked a cigarette it was with the delicate flourish of a woman. He explained to the Macleans that he helped his aged mother and sister to run the telephone exchange which was manually operated and located in a bedroom in their house. His mother had been taking calls since 1927, when the exchange first opened, with only a dozen subscribers. He himself had been away at the war, with the Highland Division in Italy.

He introduced the dog, Dìleas, which, he explained, was the

Gaelic for faithful. Marsaili didn't think that it was a very friendly-looking dog, though the MacDougalls adored it, reading to it the magazine of the Tailwaggers Club that came in its name.

The newly arrived Macleans learned that nobody called their first visitor John. He was known as *Gille Ruadh*, the red boy, because he had had red hair. It had all gone now, but he was stuck with the name, and would always be referred to as such in the Maclean household.

Gille Ruadh and the new banker were conversing in Gaelic. Evidently this was a eulogy, carefully prepared by the visitor on his way down the brae. As a boy with a full head of red hair he had had to lift his cap and salute the bank manager standing on the steps of his office, because the banker, the doctor, and the minister – next to the laird – were the most important personages in the town.

He produced a packet of Gold Flake, peeled back the silver paper and offered Alice one, then brought her a light. In all the years that he would know her, he would never call her by her first name. She would always be Mrs Maclean – or sometimes, Mistress Maclean – because his mother had taught him respect. Every Saturday night he would unzip the brown briefcase he carried under his arm, and present her with a half pound box of Black Magic for her hospitality over the previous week.

That night the new bank manager and his daughter walked Gille Ruadh up the brae, to his house. They stood conversing at the gate. His stick pointed out the light in the window, where his old mother was still taking calls past midnight. On their way down the brae the banker and his daughter could smell the honeysuckle.

2.
Rough Crossing

The first computer was still thirty years away from the island, in the hold of a vessel yet to be built. The bank office was old-fashioned, with a mahogany counter, a glass partition hiding the sloping desk where the clerk sat, writing up the ledgers. There was a supply of steel nibs in the stationery cupboard, but the clerk was using his own fountain pen; never Biro. He did, however, avail himself of the ink-stained round ruler.

The floor through to the manager's office was covered in brown battleship linoleum. The sanctum had a window overlooking Main Street. The top half bore the bank's name, and the bottom half was opaque, to preserve anonymity as customers arranged overdrafts, or explained why they could not reduce current ones.

Archie Maclean soon acquired the habit of standing by the window as he listened to his visitors. It wasn't bad manners. He was interested in the activity on Main Street, but at the same time he was listening to the voice behind him. He could hardly smile in their faces when they made a droll remark, or when an old woman

– Mrs Mary McKillop is in the visitor's chair at present – confused personal pronouns in English, calling her husband 'it', their dog 'himself'. Many times the manager had to resist the urge to burst out laughing.

Very seldom did he refuse an overdraft, whatever the size. In fact, he seemed to feel that he had to grant it because the applicant had either amused him, or saddened him with a tale of woe. Head Office was well over a hundred miles south, in an imposing building in Glasgow. The person who dealt with applications looked forward to his weekly bag of correspondence from the island. He read Archie Maclean's reports on overdrafts as if he were reading the next chapter in a thrilling adventure novel.

'Mr MacNeillage has been a faithful customer of this bank for fifty years, so I could not refuse him additional facilities of £500 last year. On the day he was due to take his cattle to the mainland a great storm – one of the fiercest in living memory – blew up. The steamer did not sail, but the sale went ahead.'

The Head Office official could see the waves breaking over the bedraggled backs of the herd standing on the island pier, waiting to be loaded on to a steamer that would not be arriving because of the gale. He could see the farmer's anxiety-ridden face at the thought that he was not going to be able to reduce his overdraft 'at present'.

What else could the official do but endorse the increased borrowing, since the money had already been spent, so he took the applications home in his briefcase, and read them to his children, to show them how English should be written.

But it wasn't English that Archie Maclean was interested in. Since coming to the island he had been obsessed with Gaelic, and he used every opportunity to improve his command of the language. When he was conversing with a customer he would stop him and ask him to explain a word, or phrase, he didn't know. And they would do likewise, because his was mainland Gaelic, unfamiliar to them in some respects. Gaelic was like whisky blends. By sampling, you could tell where the various blends or dialects came from. The island Gaelic was rich and peaty, leaving a pleasing sensation in the throat. It hadn't been contaminated by English words, like much mainland Gaelic.

The bank manager's judgement of character was based on his assessment of his customers' command of Gaelic. They could be the biggest rogues, but he overlooked everything if their Gaelic was fluent, and granted their request.

On one occasion Hector MacAndrew, the bus driver, asked for £200 to buy a second-hand car. 'Take a thousand and go for a new one,' the banker urged him magnanimously.

None of the family in the house upstairs spoke Gaelic. Alice's parents had had it, but they hadn't passed it on, like so many of their generation. They saw it as a language that held one back. At school they had been belted for answering in Gaelic, and even for using it in the playground. On the island, at the time of Archie's arrival, Gaelic was in decline, because the town, having failed to become a noted herring port, had turned itself into a tourist resort. When the steamboats began to bring the visitors, the ells of tweed were rolled out and cut with shears. English was the language of commerce. To be heard speaking Gaelic was considered illiterate. Baxter, the schoolmaster, even broke a slate over a boy's head in his exasperation at being answered back in Gaelic. The pupil had to have three stitches from Dr Murdoch's erratic needle, and his parents forbade him to use Gaelic again.

Only Marsaili showed an interest in Gaelic. She was always asking her father about place names, and he patiently translated them and tried to explain their origins. Of course many of the place names on the island were Norse, because the *Lochlannach* had been there. Once a week Marsaili was taken up the brae for a piano lesson with old Mrs Mackenzie, who had given recitals in Glasgow in her younger days, before arthritis twisted her fingers. She would put on the piano stand the music of a Gaelic song and ask her pupil to play it, and when she was satisfied she taught the banker's bright daughter the words.

'You'll need to take Gaelic when you get on a bit at school, *a Mharsaili, a gràidh*. You'll get plenty of help from your father. What a fine man he is, and what good Gaelic he has. Now next week you're going to play a very famous Gaelic song about a girl who climbs the same hill, day in, day out, to watch for the boat of her sweetheart returning, though she knows he's been lost in a storm.'

While her husband was having extra-mural classes in Gaelic down in his office, his wife was on Main Street, her shopping basket over her arm, the dog Trudie trotting on a lead at her heels, when it wasn't being carried. One of Archie Maclean's customers, embarrassed by the size of his overdraft, had brought in the West Highland puppy. As it slid down the bank counter, knocking over a pen on its stand, the banker had called his wife down from the house. The overdraft was extended, though Head Office complained.

Alice has mixed feelings about the island. Certainly it's a beautiful place, but it's getting to it. Last week, when they went back to the mainland to visit her mother, bad weather came in.

Captain Brown was on the bridge, waving to them as they went aboard to return to the island. Even at the pier Alice could feel the pitching. Immediately she went to lie down on one of the leather sofas in the saloon below, while her husband went into the bar.

The *Lochspelvie* has left the shelter of the bay, and is now being buffeted in the sound. Downstairs, Alice groans on the sofa, wishing that she could die. Upstairs, Archie is sitting at one of the small round tables with a group of farmers. The whisky glasses move about the table, as if spirits are using them to send messages. Underneath the table the sheepdogs are slithering about in sleep, muzzles on their paws. Downstairs, Alice wishes that she were being buried at sea.

The steamer puts into the first port on the island, where the figure of George Hardie looms against the stormy sky, like the ferryman on the Styx come to convey the souls. A door on the side of the vessel has been opened and George's crew are helping the terrified passengers into the small boat. One woman screams as her elegant shoe falls off and splashes into the heaving sea. As it floats away a seaman retrieves it with a boathook, tips out the water, and restores it to the frozen foot.

Archie and Alice are sailing further up the sound, into the darkness. The waves are breaking over the deck, but the Hebridean seamen walk about unconcerned, as if they are defying gravity on the tilted deck. Down in the saloon, Alice has caught sight of a passenger eating a sandwich, and has staggered to the toilet. Upstairs, Archie is hearing tales of the old times from the farmers. They have seen far worse storms. One of them, from the exposed peninsula in the south of the island, tells of the morning when, as a young shepherd at lambing time, he tried to keep upright on a storm-swept hill as he watched part of the coastline crumbling into the sea, the time-scale of Genesis being reversed in a few minutes. That morning, he told his fellow voyagers, he was more concerned with the orphaned black-faced lamb in his oilskins pocket.

Archie has a story he would never dare tell his wife. One winter's afternoon, before the Macleans came to the island, the people were huddled in the shelter of the pier building, waiting for the steamer to arrive, but there was no sign of it. A woman began to wail, because her husband was coming on the boat, which must have foundered in the ferocious weather out in the sound. There was a great deal of grief in the town that night. But next morning the *Lochspelvie* sailed into the bay. It had run into a sea loch to escape the gale, and had lain up all night, the only time that Captain Brown had been defeated by weather in the sound.

But Alice is on dry land now, walking along Main Street with her basket. Very few of the women who greet her have the courage to call her by her first name, though Alice encourages them to do so. Alice likes being a bank manager's wife. It gives her status in the community. She hears a eulogy on her husband's generosity as Joey Anderson, the butcher from Glasgow, tenderises the rump steak in the shop that the banker had helped him to buy, and when he puts the greaseproof paper parcel in Alice's basket, there is always a discount. Joey, with his striped apron wrapped round his girth, likes a bet on the horses, and in the afternoons can be heard on the phone in the back shop, laying his wagers with a city bookie.

Having asked Miss Anderson how her rheumatism was in the damp weather, Alice next went into the Island Emporium, where Neil Campbell the assistant cut the cheddar with a wire, with the precision of a surgeon amputating a limb. Sugar still came to the island in sacks, and was brought along Main Street on a barrow. Then the boy in the back shop filled the brown bags with a brass scoop. Alice marvelled at Neil's deftness in banging the bag on the counter, then folding close the top, tucking in the flaps.

Angus MacLennan, the proprietor of the Emporium, had been crowned bard at the Mod, the annual Gaelic festival, before the war, and his parchment was framed on the wall, beside the timetables of steamer excursions of past summers. Whenever Angus felt a poem coming on he would retreat into the back shop and sit on a sack of flour until he had composed it. Then he would hurry along to the bank and declaim it to Archie, who stood at the window, his back to the reciter, smiling at the hyperbolic touches in the Gaelic ode.

'That's wonderful, Angus. You must recite it at the next ceilidh.'

Alice is now at Katie's, where she has her hair done once a week. On the mainland Alice's children grew up to the noxious fumes of a home perm once a month on Saturday nights, but the bank manager's attractive wife – shiny black hair, a flawless skin, the heartthrob of several of his customers – is now bending her head to the wash-basin. In here, conversation and gossip fall with the hairs round their feet, and Alice sometimes takes home an interesting snippet to her husband. An hour later, she is sitting under the heated hood, beside Mrs Simpson, hearing what a brute her man is, drinking every night in the Ceilidh Bar. Alice puts her hand on the abused wife's arm sympathetically, though she knows that Mrs Simpson is a bitch.

Meantime Alice's daughter Marsaili is in the school at the top of the brae, getting her Gaelic lesson from Mr Robertson. He comes from another island out in the Atlantic, and because of his looks and the burr of his Gaelic, many of his pupils have crushes on him. But Marsaili is listening intently as he explains the tense system. She wants to master Gaelic, for her own sake, and because she will be the only one in the family able to converse in that language with her father. They are already very close, and nightly he tests her on twenty words of vocabulary, correcting her gently when her accent isn't quite where it should be.

'It's not a difficult language, once you get to grips with it,' he reassures her.

Her two brothers have no interest in Gaelic. The boys have inherited their father's skills as a footballer, and are still booting the ball when dusk is beginning to deepen, and the goalkeeper in his padded gloves has become a grotesque ghost between the two heaps of jerseys. The Maclean boys are naturally clever and do the minimum of homework, preferring to listen to the latest records. Their other sister Eilidh is lazy and very personable.

A fortnight before, the cargo boat from Glasgow discharged the first jukebox. It was slung ashore in a sling, handled with as much care as coffins from the steamer are handled. Swaddled in sacking, it was conveyed along Main Street on the back of a lorry to the Sea Breezes Café.

By evening Alan Fulton the electrician had rigged it up, and most of the young people in the town, including the Macleans, crowded round the lighted console, as if it contained a holy relic. A coin was inserted. A click, and the curved arm came out, lifting the small black disc from its rack.

'It'll be the death of Gaelic,' Archie told his children sadly when they had reported home on the new arrival.

'Gaelic's dead,' his wife said dismissively. 'What use is it anyway? I would much rather that Marsaili was taking French.'

This was dangerous ground that Alice had ventured out on before, but she wasn't going to retreat.

'Gaelic is at the heart of our culture,' her husband informed his family. 'It's a beautiful language, and everyone should be working to preserve it. Why would Marsaili want to speak French? She doesn't intend to go and live in France, do you, lassie?'

Marsaili agreed with a nod, though she didn't like being between her parents in an argument, especially over a subject as sensitive as Gaelic.

But as he stood at the window overlooking the bay, arguing for the preservation of his culture, Archie Maclean knew that Gaelic was on the way out. Every week there was another coffin coming off the steamer; another Gaelic speaker struck from the next census; a double line drawn on the page in the ledger next door. These old people were the precious ones, because they were the tradition bearers. They came slowly down the brae, holding on to the railing, to see the banker. They didn't want to talk to him about how much money they had in the bank, because most of them had very little, or nothing. They wanted to talk to him in Gaelic. No, that wasn't quite accurate; they wanted someone to hear them talking in Gaelic, and they knew that the banker was a good listener, standing at his window while they told him stories about their families, and about the history of the town. They told him about growing up in thatched houses at the top of the town, where the well was a quarter of a mile away and the only language was Gaelic. Their memory went far back beyond the potato blight and the hapless Prince, to the time of the Fingalian heroes.

They appreciated the way the banker stopped the conversation politely to ask them the meaning of a word, a phrase, they had used. He was learning from them. His Gaelic had been somewhat hesitant when they had first had conversations with him, because, as he told them, he hadn't had the opportunity to use his native language on the mainland.

'I couldn't have chosen a better place to come than this island, Mrs Morrison. It's got the best Gaelic in the Hebrides, and so many interesting words I haven't heard before. Go on with your story about the day your husband was building the castle, when he saw the ghost.'

Other customers who had no Gaelic would be waiting impatiently to see the manager, but the banker never dismissed Mrs Morrison or her kind. She could sit there talking all morning, and he would listen. Only once would he interrupt her, to open the door that led up the stairs, to shout up to his wife to bring down a tray of tea for two, with biscuits.

Mrs Morrison dipped her digestive into the tea, because of the state of her gums, and talked on.

'Goodness, is that the time? I'm keeping you,' she would say, eventually looking at the clock.

'You're not keeping me, Mrs Morrison,' her host said graciously. 'It's always a pleasure when you come in. Next time you're down, be sure and give me a visit – and bring that old Gaelic book you talked about. You know how interested I am in anything to do with our native tongue.'

Mrs Morrison met Harold Dawson in the passage. He was an east coast man who ran a haulage concern on the island. As Dawson went into the bank manager's office, to arrange a loan for a big new lorry, he glared at the old woman.

3.
Listening In

Gille Ruadh would climb the stairs to the bank house at ten o'
clock most evenings, a ritual that would go on for years. Most times
he brought the terrier, which lay by his chair as he sat with crossed
ankles, his effeminate hands offering the lady of the house Gold
Flake, and always bringing a flame to her from his Ronson lighter.

Gille Ruadh had a prodigious capacity for whisky, so his host
was back and forward to the drinks trolley in the dining-room,
setting the brimming glass by the ash-tray. Archie didn't care that
his visitor was costing him two bottles a week, or that he kept him
up till after midnight. Gille Ruadh was an intelligent man with very
expressive Gaelic, but before he broke into his first language to
converse with his host he always excused himself to Alice.

Gille Ruadh was also useful to the bank manager in a business
sense, supplying verbal references for customers who had applied
for overdrafts. Archie would pick up the phone in the office.

'Number please?' Gille Ruadh asked from his seat at the

exchange. But he always said to the bank manager in Gaelic, 'it's yourself.'

'I had Calum Angus MacKinnon in just now, looking for a loan for a boat. Is he trustworthy?'

There would be a pause. 'Well, they're very good fishermen.'

The banker waited expectantly.

'Shall we say that they cast their nets where they shouldn't?' Gille Ruadh added.

'You mean, in other people's beats.'

'That's right. So if it was to get around that you had given him money for a new boat, the other fishermen wouldn't be pleased.'

The banker always took his informant's advice. Sometimes the calls were even stranger.

'Put me through to Archie Beag,' the bank manager would ask, without giving the number.

'As a matter of fact he's just phoned from the call box opposite the Ceilidh Bar,' Gille Ruadh informed him. 'I wouldn't try to do business with him, with the cargo he's got in him.'

This was proof of what the bank manager had been told by several customers who came in for a Gaelic conversation. Gille Ruadh listened in to calls, as his mother did. You couldn't say anything on the line without the danger of it being repeated.

'How else did the town come to know that my daughter was expecting to a fisherman from Ayrshire?' Mrs Chisholm complained fiercely in the bank manager's office. 'Because she was foolish enough to phone home and tell us. Can you imagine what it must have been like in the wartime, with all those Admirals using the phone? That old besom up the hill must have overheard plenty of state secrets. I wouldn't be surprised if she passed them on to the Germans. They're a treacherous family, you know. You need to watch Gille Ruadh.'

But the bank manager knew that his conversations with Gille Ruadh would always remain confidential.

'My mother thinks it's a great honour for me to be coming up to the banker's house,' he announced one Saturday evening, after he had ceremoniously handed over the Black Magic.

Marsaili sniggered on the sofa. She was allowed to stay up late so that she could learn from the visitor's impeccable Gaelic.

The bank manager's relationship with Gille Ruadh was one of symbiosis, a word for which there is no equivalent in Gaelic. Archie got valuable insights into his customers from the man at the exchange, and Gille Ruadh had the prestige of being a welcome guest in the bank house, as well as getting his host's services as *fear an taighe* at ceilidhs.

When he wasn't listening into other people's calls Gille Ruadh was arranging the town's entertainment. He was Secretary of the Highland Games; and he had started a club based on age, the Forty Club, of which Archie and Alice became members. He also ran ceilidhs weekly in the summer for the visitors, and the banker introduced the acts and recited humorous poems he had written. A year after Marsaili had started Highland dancing lessons, she was persuaded to dance the Fling for the tourists while Willie Logan played his pipes.

Alice was in charge of the tea which was served at the interval. The helpers Gille Ruadh had recruited brought home baking, laying out the fantail shortbread and lethal cream sponges on the trestle table, and wielding the huge enamel teapot with the dented spout. Meantime Gille Ruadh was going round the artistes, telling them when they would appear in the second half of the programme. Marsaili couldn't do another Fling, and hadn't yet mastered the Swords, but she sang a Gaelic song about the island while her teacher accompanied her on the piano, her swollen ankles on the pedals.

After the ceilidh Gille Ruadh would bring the takings up to the bank house. Archie knew that he had deducted a sum for his own expenses, but didn't grudge him this, because he gave so much of his spare time to organising functions.

Gille Ruadh would drink half a bottle of whisky neat before being accompanied up the hill by his host and, at the weekends, by Marsaili too. They walked slowly along Main Street so that the terrier could investigate the closes, and leave his mark on the railings. The conversation between the banker and the telephone operator would be entirely in Gaelic, the stick swinging up to point out windows where local worthies lived. There was the house in Graham's Land of Mollie. Archie was expecting a story about a female, but Mollie was evidently a male, 'not all there,' Gille Ruadh explained.

Gille Ruadh told the story as they went up the brae. Mollie had been met at the top of the town with a horse and cart. Someone had pointed out that the horse looked very tired, so Mollie had decided to lighten its load by standing on the cart and putting the bale of hay on his shoulder.

'When did he die?' the banker asked, intrigued.

'He's not dead, but he doesn't come out much, except to go to the Arms.'

'Describe him,' the banker requested.

'A small stocky man, with a big drooping moustache. A brutal-looking man. He used to give his poor wife terrible beatings. We could hear her screams up at our house.'

'And nobody stopped him?' the banker asked, appalled.

'Mollie's a very strong man. One night when he was in a fight outside the Arms it took the constable and three men to hold him down, but by that time he had done the damage and broken the other man's jaw. A brute, that's what he is,' Gille Ruadh said, brandishing his stick at the high dark windows. In time Mollie would star in one of the banker's films, a brief walk-on part of him emerging from one doorway and going into the Arms fifty yards along Main Street, but sufficient to show the brutal build.

On another night Gille Ruadh's stick swept up to a tenement.

'We were living there the night the birds came.'

Years later, in her Glasgow home, when she was nostalgic about the island she had grown up in, Marsaili would recall that story told that balmy evening as the three of them stood looking up at the tenement. The windows had been left open, and about midnight the red-headed boy, sharing his bed with two brothers, heard a fluttering in the room, and then a churring sound.

'My mother had been ill, having my sister, and I thought she was going to die,' Gille Ruadh told the banker and his daughter.

But it wasn't a warning from the other world. It was a bird, and it was soon joined by dozens of others, fluttering through the open window. Gille Ruadh had lit a candle to see a small black bird with a baleful eye glaring at him from one of his boots, and twenty other birds roosting along the mantelpiece like large balls of soot. And they were still coming, until the room was filled with beating wings and calls. Gille Ruadh's father opened the door, and that let the invasion into the other rooms. Before the red-headed boy could get the window shut there were at least a hundred birds in the house, and the mother was crouched over the new baby in case they took its eyes.

But when the red-headed boy woke in the dawn, the birds had gone, as if they had been part of a collective nightmare. Other people in the tenements along Main Street had had the same invasion, and it took a day with a dozen scrubbing brushes to clean up the mess.

'What were they?' Marsaili asked in wonder.

Well, Gille Ruadh said, they had asked Dan Angus MacColl, the schoolmaster, a clever man who was known to be knowledgeable about birds. One of the them had broken its neck against a mirror, trying to get through it to the other side, and when the specimen was delivered to Dan Angus's house, he pronounced it a storm petrel.

'In fact, he gave a lecture in the hall about the birds,' Gille Ruadh recalled. 'He said that instead of complaining about the shit we had to scrub away, we should feel honoured that such shy birds should make their homes with us, even for a night.'

The retired schoolmaster, pince-nez on his nose and speaking in impeccable Gaelic, had put forward the theory that the petrel, which nested on a remote island to the west, had become disorientated in a high wind and had come into the bay instead, mistaking the red-headed boy's boots and fireplaces for their burrows.

'Did they ever come back?' Marsaili asked wistfully as they continued along Main Street, past the tenements that had rung with the calls of the lost birds.

No, they had never come back. A week later, as he was going to bed, Gille Ruadh had found a feather in one of his boots. He stopped under the streetlight and opened his wallet, handing Marsaili the white rump feather.

'It's my lucky charm,' he explained. 'I had it with me throughout the war and never came to any harm because of it.'

The feather went back into his wallet and they proceeded up the brae.

Some evenings the banker and his daughter walked along the path to the estate on the other side of the bay. The baronial mansion and ten thousand acres had been sold in the latter part of the nineteenth century by a bankrupt Maclean to a shipping magnate called Ainsworthy whose fortune had come in part from conveying reluctant emigrants from the Highland Clearances across the Atlantic.

The deadly spores of the potato blight had arrived on the island in 1845, borne on the wind or on the boots of a traveller. At that time eighteen hundred souls were crowded into the town. Though a meal depot was set up, there was not sufficient to feed the destitute, and many died of typhus and cholera in their hovels. The laird took the opportunity to ship hundreds across the Atlantic.

The banker had heard tales in his office from an old woman of her great-aunt, whose baby had died on one of the Ainsworthy

Line ships, but instead of declaring it she kept it under her shawl, because she wanted it to be buried on alien soil rather than at sea, where the creatures of the deep would eat it.

The Ainsworthys had botanists on horses with voluminous saddlebags scouring the exotic parts of the globe for the seeds of colourful shrubberies and plants to adorn their island demesne. The policies were a blaze of colour from the rhododendron bushes, and there was a fifty feet high artificial waterfall providing electricity for the chandeliers of the mansion, where the magnate entertained lavishly. Tame ducks paddled on the man-made lake, and his sixty ton sloop was tied up at the jetty which had taken fifty men six months to construct out of granite blocks.

Every Sunday the Colonel and his family were rowed across the bay in a special 'church boat', to occupy the screened-off pew. He owned the town as well, and had built the hall, with a library of books, philosophical and literary, to improve the minds of the locals, many of whom spoke Gaelic only, and had no reading skills in any language. During the Great War daily telegrams from Reuters laid out on the table informed the islanders of battles won and lost. Symmers the minister read them out at nine o' clock in the evening, standing by the fountain across from the hall, whose arching water came from the penis of the little cherub. If a church elder was met in his Sunday black on a week day, then he was delivering a telegram about a death in France or Belgium.

Ten years before Archie Maclean and family had arrived on the island, the Colonel's great grandson had removed the roof from the mansion to avoid death duties, and because the place was riddled with damp. He abandoned his home and went to live in the dower house a mile away, itself a substantial place of twenty rooms. The locals lifted off the mahogany doors from the derelict mansion, and stripped the lead from the roof.

As the banker and his daughter wandered through the perfumed grounds of the abandoned Ainsworthy residence on a summer evening, Marsaili received a lesson on the foibles and frailties of man and his earthly mansions. The dozen gardeners had gone, and the electricity plant rusted by the waterfall. With no billhooks to hack it back, the ponticum was out of control, even crossing the main road on to crofts.

They stood together at the entrance, where no locals had dared to go in the heyday of the house. The banker pointed out the fancy tracery above the windows, the sparrow hawk's nest in the turret.

'They couldn't speak a word of Gaelic, Marsaili, yet they owned the town, and the people too, they thought. No wonder there's so little of the language left.'

Was the banker a hypocrite, or just polite? When Colonel Ainsworthy's thin, tight-lipped great grandson came into the bank he gave him a chair and sat opposite him. The heir talked about his investments. His broker in London had told him to hold on to Cunard, but what did the banker think? The banker thought that he should, though he didn't follow the stock exchange. The tight-lipped man with the English voice complained about money and went his way along Main Street, where, unlike his father, nobody saluted him. The banker watched him climbing into his Land Rover, out of which a pair of oars was protruding.

4.
Man o' War

One Saturday evening after Gille Ruadh had unzipped his briefcase and handed his hostess her Black Magic, he also produced something for Archie Maclean. The banker unwrapped the tissue paper to reveal a block of dark wood. Marsaili began to giggle as her father, too polite to ask questions, turned the block in his hands.

'That's a very special piece of wood,' the visitor said enigmatically.

'Did it grow on the island?' Archie asked.

'It wasn't found on the island, but *off* it.'

The banker turned to his daughter for help, handing her the block. She noticed the small holes.

'Has it been in the sea?' she asked.

'Clever girl,' Gille Ruadh said. 'It came from the bay. It's part of the galleon.'

Archie had heard about the galleon long before he had come to the island. He had read that in the late summer of 1588 a 'Great

Ship of Spaigne' had come into the bay, its sails in tatters, its rigging heaped on the deck. In the ferocious storm other ships from the Armada had been wrecked on the coast of Ireland, the noblemen on board dragged to the bottom by the weight of the gold chains round their necks. But this ship had managed to find the shelter of the sound in the Hebrides, to turn her rudder into the bay that September day.

It needed water for the wounded, and wood to repair the deck and spars. In exchange for these necessities the local chief had borrowed a contingent of the Spanish soldiers in his dispute with the chief of a neighbouring island. The plumes in their hats and powder-horns on their chests had terrified the islanders, their confidence already shaken by the cannon that the chief had also borrowed from the Spanish galleon.

Then, shortly before it was due to sail home, the repaired ship was wrecked by an explosion and fire. Archie Maclean had read several explanations. One was that the wife of the local chief was jealous because her husband was paying court to a beautiful Spanish princess on board the galleon. The betrayed wife turned for assistance to a local witch, who conjured up a pack of fairy cats and sent them to terrorise the Spanish crew. One of the cats apparently chased a seaman into the ship's magazine, where sparks from its fairy fur ignited a gunpowder keg.

There was a more prosaic explanation. The island chief had heard that this was the treasure ship of the Armada, with a fabulous cargo of golden ducats. He had the ship blown up, expecting to salvage the chests of money, but by the time he got near to the burning hulk it was already sinking.

Men had gone down in primitive diving bells to try to salvage the treasure, and had drowned in the attempt. Then, in 1928, a bounty hunter had arrived at the Hebridean Hotel above the bay. His name was Colonel Aubrey Fawcett, and he was accompanied by a young lady, Miss Wendy Staples.

'You actually met him, John?' the banker asked.

'I showed him up to his room,' Gille Ruadh said proudly. 'I was the assistant hall porter at the time. Room Eight it was, overlooking the bay, with a private bathroom. Miss Staples got Room Ten next door, smaller, but with a bathroom too.'

The former porter described the pile of trunks that had come off the steamer for the pair – six in all – weighing down the hotel cart to the extent that the horse had strained its heart, hauling the load up the brae, and had had to be retired to a croft.

'Why so much stuff?' the intrigued banker asked.

'Well, they were going to stay for a long time,' Gille Ruadh explained.

The Colonel asked for a big table to be brought up to his room, and he sat at it in the bay window, poring over charts of the bay he had found in some library or somewhere. Gille Ruadh looked coyly at his shoes. 'He asked me to invest.'

'To invest, John?' the banker prompted gently.

'To invest in his salvage company. The Man o' War, it was called. You bought shares in it, to help finance the work, and you got a big payment when the treasure was found.'

'And did you invest, John?' It was an equally gentle question.

'I had thirty pounds in the bank here and I was tempted, but my mother wouldn't allow me. She said she didn't like the sound of Colonel Fawcett's voice.'

'Oh – so she *met* him, John.'

'No, she never met him, but she heard him often enough. He would come on the phone to her from the hotel and ask her to put him through to numbers in London. He even wanted calls to America.'

The banker smiled as he pictured the scene: Gille Ruadh's mother plugged into the private conversation between the swashbuckling treasure seeker and the rich Yank he was trying to persuade to invest in the Man o' War scheme.

A week after the Colonel and his pretty assistant had installed themselves in adjacent rooms in the Hebridean Hotel, the salvage barge came into the bay. An old woman, Martha McKellaig, who lived in one of the slum tenements, had gone along Main Street one evening to see if she could scrounge a few fish from one of the boats at the pier. When she saw the gigantic figure with the bulbous head and heavy boots coming up the steps she thought she was seeing a monster from the deep, such as her husband, who had sailed on schooners, had described in his graphic Gaelic. Martha had died of a heart attack on a bench as someone was trying to explain to her in Gaelic that she was seeing her first diver.

The barge was also equipped with a pump which sucked up the silt from the sea bed and spewed it on to the deck, over a series of grilles, where it was shaken in the search for artefacts, before being spewed back over the other side of the barge. The slobbering noise went on late into the evening during that summer, and guests up in the Hebridean Hotel complained that their children couldn't sleep because of the racket of the pump and the arc lamps shining into their waterfront rooms.

'But the Colonel and his companion got to sleep all right, John?' the banker prompted.

Gille Ruadh glanced at Marsaili, then began to speak in Gaelic quickly, so that the conversation was confined to himself and his host. The bathroom had connecting doors, because the two rooms had been designed to serve as a suite for big families, or a party. The thumping noise coming from the Colonel's room suggested that he was trying out a new type of suction pump. The young Gille Ruadh, with a full head of red hair, and his shoes shining, was standing in the hall below, listening for the bells of guests ringing for night-caps. Instead he heard a female calling out on the first floor.

For the first time in this private conversation the very fluent Gille Ruadh was stuck for a Gaelic word, not because he had forgotten it, but because there was no equivalent for the English.

'One of the maids told me that when the Colonel left and they turned the mattress to air it, they found over forty French letters.'

'He must have had some stamina,' the banker suggested, again in Gaelic, with his daughter watching him suspiciously.

He had had a great deal of stamina, Gille Ruadh agreed, safely reverting to English. He had his breakfast at six-thirty, always two kippers, two eggs, and extra toast. Then he had his whisky flask filled up for the day before the hotel car took him down to Main Street, where he was shipped out on to the barge. Gille Ruadh gave an account of the flamboyant bounty hunter's garb. A checked plus-fours suit; a matching Inverness cape; brown brogues with serrated tongues; a two-way hat. At one o' clock Gille Ruadh or another member of staff from the hotel took a basket covered with a white cloth down the brae to the steps, where it was conveyed out to the barge. This was the Colonel's lunch, usually cold chicken, bread, a bottle of wine. He sat on a folding chair, watching the vibrating grille as he ate. He never took his eyes off the grille for a second, not even to draw the cork.

'He was terrified that if gold coins were brought up, the crew would steal them,' Gille Ruadh explained.

It was more than suspicion. It was certainty. Colonel Fawcett had found a document in some library that convinced him that this was the Armada treasure ship. The chests would have long since rotted, of course, but he sat on the deck of the barge that balmy summer, gnawing a chicken leg, convinced that at any moment golden coins would rain down from the suction hose on to the grille, where they would leap for joy, so many of them that some of them would fall overboard again, but they would be retrieved by the diver who moved with an axe in the murky depths below.

'You'll get your investment back a thousand fold!' the prospectus of the Man o' War Enterprise sang from the glossy page. 'Museums and collectors all over the world are waiting to bid for

stories from an island   39

the ducats we are about to raise from the bay of this lovely Hebridean island, a bay that has sheltered and preserved the wreck of this great treasure ship for nearly four hundred years.'

Gille Ruadh declined the offer. Instead he continued to take the treasure hunter's lunch down to him, and his mother continued to listen into his calls as she wielded the plugs and pushed the keys in the manual exchange up the hill, sometimes going next door to put on pots of herring and potatoes for supper between trunk calls. She listened to the prospector, and she laughed gleefully.

'Did he find anything?' Marsaili asks, the first time she has spoken this evening, sitting thoughtfully, with the block of Armada timber in her lap, the hacks of the salvor's axe having bitten deep. Even Dìleas seems to be listening intently to his master's tale.

'They found rusted swords, that sort of thing. The diver said that he had located the barrel of a cannon, but when he was lowered again it turned out to be a tree trunk.'

'So there was no gold, John?' the banker asked. 'I suppose the locals wouldn't have left it lying at the bottom of the bay for all those years. They've got a great love of money on this island. If they could blow the safe in the bank below and help themselves – and get away with it, of course – they would.'

The visitor was smiling, not at his host's description of his fellow islanders, which he would have agreed with. He was smiling at the memory. One day, after he had taken the Colonel's lunch basket down, he was lingering on Main Street, having a smoke and talking to someone, when there was a shout from the barge.

There, among the vibrating small stones on the grille, was a coin.

The bank manager left his guest to his dramatic moment. As he sat in his chair, with the light fading on the bay which was the subject of the story, Archie Maclean was thinking of the Fingalian tales of old. Apparently they took nights to tell, but the narrator was always word-perfect, and never deviated from the dramatic line. Gille Ruadh came from this tradition in which there was all the time in the world to tell a tale, because, in a sense, you never reached the end of it. Long after the speaker had stopped, it would resonate in the heads of the listeners, embellished and dramatised, until their version passed into the repertoire and became word-perfect too. This was another of the beauties of the Gaelic language, the way it treated time. So Gille Ruadh picked up the packet of Gold Flake, and offered the lady of the house one, with an accompanying flame. Meantime the host has gone through to the trolley for another brimming dram for the guest, and when he had swallowed a mouthful, the tale teller resumed.

'They employed a local man called Dodie MacFarlane on the barge. He was a very fly man, was Dodie. I was in school with him and you couldn't turn your back on him, otherwise he would have your bread and cheese out of your desk and into his own mouth. Anyway, Dodie was on board the barge, doing as little as possible, as usual, and getting well paid for it. He must have thought to himself, if they don't find anything soon, they'll tow the barge away and I'll be out of a job. Any man who can take the dinner out of your desk while you're sitting at it could certainly toss a coin on a grille without Colonel Fawcett noticing.'

It was the shout of one of the men that Gille Ruadh had heard on shore, as he idled with a local before going back up to his duties at the Hebridean Hotel. The Colonel upset his bottle of wine as he lurched for the coin, actually catching it in mid-air above the grille. He scratched away the dirt with his nail and saw the glitter of gold. That afternoon the Colonel commandeered the post office, firing off telegrams to his shareholders – and to the newspapers.

TREASURE FOUND! was the headline in all the next day's papers. The Hebridean Hotel couldn't accommodate the journalists and photographers who came from all over the world. Gille Ruadh made a lot of money, giving them the fabulous history of the galleon, dragged to the bottom by the weight of its treasure. As for the

Colonel, the photographers were out on the barge around him as he held up the coin. Undoubtedly it was a ducat. He didn't need to send it to an expert for authentication; the books he had up in his room told him that. From the reign of Philip, freshly minted to pay the Armada. The photographers wanted to catch the treasure hunter biting into the coin, but he had a better idea.

Miss Staples was brought out to the barge. She was wearing a sailor suit and fetching nautical cap as she posed with the coin on her palm, a pin-up photo that was reproduced round the world. Within two days, Gille Ruadh's mother was taking no more calls for Colonel Fawcett at the Hebridean Hotel. She listened to their hysterical pledges that they were putting a cheque for a thousand pounds sterling into the next day's post as payment for shares in the Man o' War Syndicate. The elderly woman pulled the plug on the subscribers, and went to see how the potato and herring supper was coming along on the stove.

'What about this block of wood?' Marsaili wanted to know.

'I'll tell you about it some other night,' its owner promised. 'Dìleas is getting tired, aren't you, boy?' he spoke to the dog stretched out at his shoes.

5.
Calling the Tune

On summer evenings when Marsaili and her father were walking
along Main Street, they would hear music coming from the Ceilidh
Bar close to the pier. Marsaili stood on tiptoe to look over the
engraved window. Alasdair MacTavish was playing for his customers, fingering out Gaelic tunes on the piano accordion. One couple
were even up dancing between the tables, her head on his shoulder.

'If you weren't too young I would take you in to hear him,'
Archie told his daughter. 'There's no one better.'

Marsaili mentioned Alasdair's name the next time she was up
at Mrs Mackenzie's for her piano lesson, and while she practised
scales she heard the story.

Old MacTavish, the proprietor of the Ceilidh Bar and of the
hotel of which it was a part, was a brilliant piper who had taken the
Clasp at the Northern Meeting against one of the legendary
Macphersons of Invershin, playing *I Got a Kiss of the King's Hand*.
He bought his son Alasdair a set of miniature pipes and coached

him himself, making him walk up and down the public bar while the other boys were up playing football in the park.

Then one stormy night an Irish trawler ran into the bay for shelter. The crew came ashore to the Ceilidh Bar for company and whisky. The skipper opened the black box he had with him and produced a small melodeon. Its harmony filled the bar as he fingered out a selection of Irish reels. It wakened the boy in his bedroom at the top of the hotel.

'He thought he was dreaming, having never heard such wonderful music, and he went downstairs to see what instrument it was,' Mrs Mackenzie explained to her pupil.

The sleepy barefooted boy is standing in the doorway of the public bar. He sees the skipper in the cheese-cutter hat and sea boots turned down at the thighs sitting by the fire, squeezing the delicate inlaid box between his large hands.

The Irishman notices him and calls him over.

'Go and get your pipes, boy,' MacTavish tells his son.

His bare feet walk the boards of the bar as he plays a medley of Gaelic airs as the drinkers clap and toast him.

'Try this,' the man from Donegal says, handing the boy the melodeon.

As his fingers touch the buttons Alasdair knows that this is the instrument he wants to play. They listen in silence as he plays the same selection of Gaelic airs he has just played on the pipes.

'Remember, this boy can't read a note of music, and he's never touched a melodeon in his life before,' Mrs Mackenzie tells Marsaili.

Alasdair handed back the melodeon, but the skipper pushed it away.

'That was made for you, son.'

The boy lugged the melodeon upstairs and was sitting fingering out more tunes when his father came up in his frightening shoes.

'You're a piper, not a bloody melodeon player,' he reminded his son, snatching away the instrument.

The boy heard the front door slamming. He crossed to the window and saw his father out on the street. He swung the melodeon and flung it out, towards the lights of the Irish trawler.

'So how did he become an accordionist?' Marsaili asked, mystified.

'I'll show you,' Mrs Mackenzie said, going to a cupboard and taking out a case. She stood the red lacquered melodeon on the table. 'This was my father's. He used to play it in this very room. What musical ability I have came from him. So, I heard about what had happened with the Irish trawler, and one afternoon when Alasdair was coming home from school I rapped the window. He came in and had his first lesson on this.' She put her hand on the melodeon, as if blessing it. 'Fifteen minutes only, because then he had to go down and play the pipes for his father.'

The deception went on for years, until Alasdair had outgrown the miniature pipes. One afternoon his father brought his own set down to the public bar. They were black ebony, with silver mounts, red tassels hanging from the drones.

'These are two hundred years old,' MacTavish told his son. 'They're yours now.'

He was waiting for the young man to lift them from the case and put them against his shoulder.

'I'm sorry, father, but I don't want to go on with the pipes.'

'What do you mean? You're the best piper I've ever heard, and I've competed against the best. If you and I were in for the Gold Medal at the Northern Meeting this year I know who would win.'

'His father thought he was just going through an awkward phase and would come round in time,' Mrs Mackenzie explained to Marsaili. 'But the next week Alasdair came up here and asked me if he could borrow the melodeon because he wanted to play for a dance in the hall.'

It started at nine. Alasdair was sitting on the platform, with one of his school friends on drums, his friend Strathspey Mackintosh on fiddle. By ten o' clock the hall was crowded with dancers, many of whom had been warming up in the Arms and the Ceilidh Bar.

'Someone told his father that Alasdair was playing in the hall,' Mrs Mackenzie said.

Alasdair is playing a Gaelic waltz when he sees his father in the doorway. The big man who can lift a beer barrel by himself has his hands on either side, as if in rage he's trying to push apart the lintels. The dancers are turning in front of him. Then he's gone. Alasdair goes home in trepidation that night, expecting to find the key turned against him, his possessions in the street. He sees a light in the public bar and looks through the curtains. His father is sitting by the fire, the pipes across his knees, staring at them.

'I'm sorry,' Alasdair says.

'Who taught you to play like that?' his father wants to know.

'Of course he wanted to protect me, but he didn't want to tell a lie,' Mrs Mackenzie told Marsaili.

'I've been getting lessons from Mrs Mackenzie,' Alasdair revealed to his father.

'You won't have time for lessons, now you've left school. I need your help to run this place. You'll start tomorrow, taking the stores up from the pier.'

He trundled the barrow of sacks of flour and crates of beer along Main Street to the hotel, and by the end of that week he was too tired to go up the hill to see Mrs Mackenzie.

'Then he phoned me,' she told Marsaili, who was now utterly absorbed in the story.

That Saturday night Alasdair came in at the back of ten, after the bar had closed. The door was open and he noticed something gleaming on the floor by the fading fire. It was a piano accordion, a beautiful thing of white keys and silverwork. He was touching the notes when his father spoke behind him.

'If you're going to play the accordion, at least play a decent instrument.'

Within a month Alasdair was doing dances at the weekend on the island. Then he got bookings on the mainland.

'They soon had a minibus to drive all over Scotland,' Mrs Mackenzie recalled. She touched the gold mesh on her wireless as if it were an icon. 'When he played his first broadcast the tears were streaming down my face because he'd composed a tune, *Mrs Aileen Mackenzie*, a waltz. I'll teach you it,' she promised Marsaili. 'It's a beautiful tune.'

The Alasdair MacTavish Band consisted of himself on accordion, Donald Brown on a second box, Strathspey Mackintosh on fiddle, and Donnie Munro on drums. They brought a new and exhilarating sound to the dance floors of Scotland and beyond.

'I went down to Glasgow to a dance they were playing at,' Mrs Mackenzie reminisced to her pupil. 'It was the annual gathering for this island, and there were six hundred people in the St Andrews Halls. Alasdair and his band were in MacTavish tartan dinner jackets and bow ties up on the platform. They looked so professional, I was so proud of them. The women were all in long dresses, and I didn't see one man who wasn't in a kilt, or trews.

'They played us into the hall in the Grand March. Then he called a Gaelic waltz. And do you know what he did? He unstrapped his accordion and came down off the platform to dance with his old teacher, leaving the rest of the band to play the tune he had written for me. I was so proud, I felt I was floating above the floor, and he was such a graceful dancer. I thought, if it hadn't been for my father's little red melodeon neither of us would be here now.'

Alasdair and his band started making records in London, and they sold so well that the musicians were invited across to Canada for a coast-to-coast tour. Expatriate Highlanders and the descendants of people who had been cleared more than a century before from the island by the Ainsworthy Line were on the dance floors of Montreal, Toronto and Vancouver. Beautiful sophisticated women came up to Alasdair and asked him for requests. He played Gaelic waltzes, with tunes from the old island, and he obliged with an Eightsome Reel, during which one of the women flung away her shoe with its broken heel and continued in her stockinged feet because she didn't want to lose a bar of the exhilarating music.

Glasses of whisky were placed on the piano for the band, and were emptied by the interval. Liquor seemed to make them even better musicians, and when they introduced a little jazz into a Canadian Barn Dance the people on the floor went wild.

Alasdair insisted that he and his band stayed in the best hotels, with room service. After dances they were invited to parties in private houses. One night in Toronto Alasdair, who had already drunk a great deal over the course of the evening, went through to the kitchen to find the ice-box for a few cubes for his whisky, because he was getting used to Canadian habits. His hostess came in while he was at the sink.

'You played so wonderfully well tonight, I'm still floating,' she told him. 'I'm going to take that last Gaelic waltz you played to bed with me.' She looked at him as she snapped her cigarette lighter. 'On second thoughts, why not the player?'

When Alasdair was playing an encore in the heat of Adelaide, he received a telegram, informing him that his father had died. He flew home for the delayed funeral, and played his father's pipes at the graveside.

That night his mother told him that she could no longer subsidise his band, whose fees hadn't looked at the expenses of the quality hotels, the first class travel, where his accordion occupied a seat.

'You'll need to come off the road and run the hotel, now that your father's gone.'

So Archie Maclean and Marsaili heard him playing in his own bar on a summer evening, when they were walking along Main Street. When he played a Gaelic waltz, his own sadness as well as his genius was in it.

6.
Espresso

Every Monday morning Joe Bonelli came along Main Street with a grey canvas sack containing his takings which he slid over the bank counter to the teller before going into the manager's office. Far from having an overdraft, Joe had thousands in his account. His conversations with his banker were personal, not financial, and Archie Maclean stood at the window, looking along Main Street as he listened to his visitor's story.

The well-built little Italian had come to Glasgow to work in the café of a compatriot, and had fallen in love with one of the daughters. While serving a kilted customer, Joe had been told of an island in the Hebrides that had never tasted ice cream. The man wrote down the name of the island. Joe arrived off the steamer in 1937 with a cardboard suitcase in his hand, his bride on his arm, and a recipe for ice cream in his head.

The Bonellis took a lease of Macinnes the tailor's shop on Main Street, where the mentally retarded apprentice had sat cross-legged in the window, sewing stitches that the machine with the treadle which his boss worked at his back couldn't better. Macinnes had taken a stroke while cutting out a waistcoat, and his widow couldn't keep the business going. The sewing-machine went for scrap and the apprentice was sent to the asylum on the mainland.

The Bonellis rented the flat above as well as the shop. After they had scrubbed out the shop, Mrs Bonelli, who had the dark beauty of her country, made curtains. When the Reverend Skinner passed away they went to the manse sale and bought an assortment of chairs and tables, and cardboard boxes of mismatching cutlery. The Sea Breezes Café became a popular venue. Elderly locals came in to gossip in Gaelic over the first cups of coffee of their lives. The café was busy throughout the summer with trippers consuming fluted dishes of ice cream and writing postcards before the whistle of the steamer called them back. They left sixpences under the saucers and the Bonellis saved them in a gallon whisky bottle with a slot at the neck.

In the winter Mrs Bonelli made a fire with wood she had gathered from the shore, and locals sheltered in the cosy café as the sea broke over the railings. Then came the war and the town became an important naval base. The Bonellis had lost a lot of business when the excursion steamers were withdrawn because of the U-boat threat. However, the naval personnel frequented the café, with WRNS sitting over cups of tea with their dates.

One quiet afternoon two men carrying a sling of tools between them came into the café. Joe didn't recognise them as locals. They laid the tools across a table, and one of them turned the key in the door and flipped round the Closed sign while the other one pulled the curtains.

'What are you doing?' Joe demanded.

They were pushing aside the tables and tearing up the linoleum.

'I'm going for the police,' Joe told them as he made for the door.

'We *are* the police,' one of the men informed him, inserting a crowbar between floorboards and levering them up with a screech of nails.

'What are you wanting in here?' Joe asked, getting even more frightened.

'We have reason to believe you have a transmitter in here and are sending messages to Italy,' one of them said.

'Who told you this nonsense?' Joe demanded to know.

But one of the men was now under the floor, searching with a torch. They went through to the back shop, ripping up the linoleum there also.

'My wife is resting,' Joe protested as they went up the stairs.

They pulled her out of the bed and made her stand by the window in her nightdress as they ripped open the mattress with a knife, scattering the horsehair. They lifted the floorboards and knocked the walls with a hammer.

'I told you, there's nothing here,' Joe said, close to tears, seeing years of work ruined. 'You *must* put this right.'

'You're coming with us,' one of the men said.

They struggled with Joe and his wife joined in, beating the intruders with her fists as they got her husband's hands behind his back, pushed him down the stairs, marched him across Main Street, down the steps and into a boat. One local man who tried to intervene was knocked unconscious with a tool.

Joe Bonelli was to spend the rest of the war interned as an alien. His wife wasn't allowed any contact with him. She borrowed tools from Matheson the joiner and put the floorboards back in the café. She tacked down the ripped linoleum and set up the tables and chairs again, then turned the notice on the door: OPEN.

Joe was in a detention camp on the Isle of Man, a grim place. The locals shouted at them and threw stones.

'All that kept me from hanging myself from the rafters, as some others did, was the thought that I would see Stella and this place again,' he told his bank manager.

The worst day was when he received word that his cousin Guido, who had a café in Edinburgh, was among those lost when the *Arandora Star* was torpedoed, carrying Italian deportees to Canada.

Stella received many proposals from naval personnel during the war years, when she ran the café single-handed, but she declined all of them, including the invitation from a Rear Admiral to dine with him in the Hebridean Hotel, which the navy had requisitioned for its officers and where there was no shortage of food or drink. Instead she rationed the coffee and slept alone upstairs in the room whose floorboards she had nailed back after her husband's arrest.

A month after the end of the war Joe came back on the steamer. He had coffee in the café with his wife. Then they went upstairs, hand in hand.

'Italians love big families,' he told the banker as he sat in the swivel chair. 'There were eleven in ours, by the same mother. I said to my wife, we should have had a son at least by now but they put me away for six years.'

At thirty eight – a difficult age – Stella became pregnant, and went about the café singing love songs of her country as she helped her husband. On the night of her contractions Joe was down in the darkened café, on his knees by the new espresso coffee machine, praying for a son. At three in the morning, when he had fallen asleep between two chairs, he heard an infant crying and rushed up the stairs.

'I thought, a son – at last,' he told Archie Maclean. 'And then I saw the naked little thing. Stella said, don't worry, Joe, there's still time.'

But there were no more children. The girl was a beauty like her mother. The locals had stood by his wife during his internment and he gave his daughter a Gaelic name. Cairistiona Stella Bonelli and Marsaili Maclean went up the brae to school in the mornings, their satchels on their backs, taking each other's hands to cross the road. When they came down after three they went along to the café for a slider. Joe wanted to give it to Marsaili for nothing, but her mother insisted that she pay for it.

Cairistiona and Marsaili competed to get gold stars in their jotters from Miss MacColl, and one warm afternoon when they were going down the brae to their sliders Cairistiona confined to her friend that she had decided to be a doctor. Since Marsaili was going to be a vet their friendship wasn't tested.

On late summer evenings Mrs Bonelli took Cairistiona and Marsaili along the path that led away from the town to the lighthouse overlooking the sound. Mrs Bonelli had a basket over her arm as she led the two girls down a track, to show them where the mushrooms grew, telling them that her family had picked them for a living in Italy.

'You have to know what you're looking for. Some of them are poisonous,' she warned.

They picked the ones she pointed out, and Cairistiona and Marsaili carried the basket between them on the way home along the path, towards the lights of the town through the foliage. One evening Archie Maclean up at his tower window filmed the trio. It was one of his more atmospheric efforts, a slow pan from the lighted clock showing nine, to the two girls in white socks and sandals, bearing the basket of yellow treasure between them while the shapely Italian woman, a scarf wrapped round her head, walked in front.

Mrs Bonelli sent most of the mushrooms on the steamer to a restaurant in London, but kept back some as a treat. The chanterelles floated like yellow flowers in the olive oil in the pan, and the girls ate them with spoons from floral plates in the shut café.

Marsaili and Cairistiona followed the lorry that conveyed the first jukebox to the Sea Breezes Café in 1959. Joe had thought long and hard about getting one, but his wife pointed out that it would bring in the local teenagers.

Marsaili was allowed to go along to the café on Friday night, with five shillings in her pocket for her selection of music. The café was always crowded. Willie McSporran, whose hair had always been cut by his father, using an inverted bowl, now persuaded 'Boots' Jamieson, the barber who went round the island on a motorbike, to change his style. 'Boots' had sellotaped the page from the magazine that Willie had given him, and painstakingly wielded his rough clippers to reproduce the first Duck's Arse style on the island. Not content, Willie had sent away for a long jacket and drainpipe trousers, and he jived to the deafening jukebox while Cairistiona and Marsaili supped ice cream with long spoons.

Joe and his wife loved the new atmosphere of their café. The espresso machine was busy all night, and Mrs Bonelli carried the glass cups of coffee to the tables occupied by the young people of the town, smoking and laughing as Willie McSporran's knees went in and out, in and out to Chuck Berry.

'The jukebox was the best buy I ever made,' Joe told his bank manager. 'In fact I've ordered a newer model. It should be coming off the cargo boat from Glasgow next Thursday.'

'Do you need an overdraft till you get the money back for it?' the banker enquired discreetly. He knew that he had to put the question for professional reasons, though the Bonellis had over three thousand pounds in a savings account, with good interest, as well as a healthy balance in their business account.

'No, no, Archie, we're fine. And I'm going to get a new coffee machine while I'm at it – one that puts froth on the meelk,' he added with a smile.

'That's a very clever daughter you have,' the banker complimented him.

'She's wonderful,' the father said, blowing a kiss. 'Even when the jukebox is going full blast she's sitting upstairs, reading. When I tell her to close the book and rest she says, I want to be a doctor, so I've got to study.'

7.
The London Scottish

This afternoon the bank manager's chair was occupied by a
tall distinguished-looking man in a tailored tweed jacket and
regimental tie, his two-way hat lying on the desk, beside the
substantial dram that Archie had poured for him. Major James
(Jamie) Farquhar was explaining to his bank manager how he came
to be on the island, and he was in no hurry to tell his story.

Two years after the end of the war the steamer had brought the
biggest car ever seen on the island. It was a Lagonda, with gleaming
bumpers and red leather, taking up most of the deck space between
the wheelhouse and the bow. Captain Brown himself went down
to tell the crew to handle it carefully. The mudguards were protected
with sacks before it was swung ashore in the net, the mate shouting
instructions in Gaelic to the man at the controls of the derrick.

As the vehicle settled on its voluptuous springs a woman came
down the gangway. She looked as if she were going to a ball, not
stepping ashore on a Hebridean pier. The owner of the Lagonda

followed her, dressed in red tweed plus-fours, with a jaunty cap. They weren't man and wife. She was Lady Annabel Crosbie-Ellis, and Major James (Jamie) Farquhar had run away with her, leaving two families totalling eight children and distraught partners behind. The Lagonda hadn't crossed the Scottish border before her children were made wards of court; before his plate was being unscrewed from the chambers where he had practised as a barrister.

They had headed for the west coast and had the Lagonda loaded on to the steamer because his father had rented a lodge on the island when Jamie was a boy, with a keeper to teach his son how to shoot woodcock. The car was driven off the pier and disappeared up the brae out of town.

'Where are we going?' Lady Annabel enquired. She had felt queasy coming up the sound on the steamer, even on this calm day, and was missing her children, though they had spent most of the time in the care of a nanny, only being paraded for the parents before dinner.

'We'll find an hotel,' her lover reassured her.

She was making her mouth up in the mirror of a gold compact as he drove. It was one of the most beautiful faces in England and had featured in the Tatler the year she was presented at court, when the man beside her, still a law student at Cambridge, was drilling with the London Scottish as a Territorial. They had met at a regimental dance. The Major's wife was not keen on reels, so he was searching for a partner for the Eightsome when he saw this beautiful woman with red hair crossing the floor. As he birled her on his arm he looked into her eyes and knew that this was the person he wanted to spend the rest of his life with.

By the time the Lagonda reached the summit of the hill the radiator was steaming. They sat on the heather bank, smoking as they admired the view. There was a village in the hollow below, beside a sea loch.

'Isn't it charming?' Annabel said, pointing to the church with its stocky spire. But the Major was looking at the house standing on the opposite shore. The Georgian property embowered among trees came with three hundred acres of arable and hill. It had been on the market for two years because it needed so much doing to it. There was no electricity, no hot water system, and the drains stank in summer. Having looked through the windows, Farquhar phoned his London lawyer from the call box in the village and asked him to find out what the agent wanted for the place. He hung about outside the box in the warmth, waiting for a reply.

'They want six thousand,' the lawyer shouted down the poor line which was being monitored by Gille Ruadh's mother. 'Listen, Jamie, don't do anything hasty. A holiday on an island like that's all very well, but settling down there? Is this what Annabel wants?'

Farquhar looked out of the small pane at his lover dozing in the Lagonda.

'She likes it here.'

'After Surrey?' the lawyer enquired dubiously. 'You're both going to miss civilisation.'

If the lawyer hadn't been in the London Scottish with him, Farquhar would have taken exception to his remark.

'Maybe they'll take five and a half, since the place has been on the market so long,' Farquhar suggested.

'I'll try them, but I think you're doing the wrong thing. Where's your income going to come from?'

'I'll farm the place.'

There was a distinct laugh. 'But you don't know anything about farming.'

'I can learn.'

'I'm worried about you using so much capital, considering what the separation's going to cost you. I know Helena's a wealthy woman in her own right, but you're the guilty party, and she'll want revenge.'

'Yes, but I'll get my mother's money,' Farquhar pointed out.

His mother, who was in her sixties, was living in an hotel in Harrogate, having been forced out of her spa on the continent because of the war. She was furious at the shame of her only son having run off with somebody else's wife, and when he'd phoned her, she had asked plainly how she was going to face people again. But he knew that she wouldn't cut him off.

On their first night in the house by the loch they slept on the mildewed horsehair mattress in the brass-framed bed.

'What's that pattering noise?' Annabel asked, sitting up.

'Rain on the roof. Go to sleep, darling.'

'It's coming from *inside* the walls.'

He had heard that sound before, at Cassino, where the shelling had sent the rats frantic.

'What is it?' she asked again.

'A mouse. Nothing to worry about.'

'I can't *bear* mice.'

She dressed and insisted that he drive her to the hotel in the village. He had to hammer on the door before the proprietor came down, grumbling. But he was ingratiating after he had drawn the bolts and saw who the nocturnal visitors were.

'I'm not moving back into that house until every mouse has been cleared out,' Annabel gave her ultimatum to her lover as the hotelier picked up her case.

Next day he phoned a firm on the mainland. That evening a battered van was dumped on the pier from the steamer. The ratcatcher was dressed in the battle-dress he had worn in the Western Desert where he had laid thousands of land-mines for the Afrika Korps.

'How do you get rid of the buggers?' the Major asked helplessly.

The man opened the back of the van and lifted out a bucket of small fish.

'Pilchards,' he said in a voice ruined by Capstan Full Strength. 'They love pilchards. Have you got any old newspapers?'

The Major brought the bundle of *Times* that arrived by post from London. The ratcatcher made up small parcels of fish and powder from a tin, leaving them in the loft and among the outhouses.

'Don't touch them,' he warned. 'There's poison in them. I'll be back in a week.'

A few days later, when the Major went into the scullery, he saw a rat dragging itself across the stone floor. He hit it with a poker, then went through for a shovel.

'Rats are clever little bastards,' the catcher informed him when he'd returned from clearing an infested farm in the south of the island. 'The old ones get the young ones to taste the bait. I'll need to put more down.'

Every day the Major was lunching with his lover at the hotel, assuring her that the battle with the mice was being won, and that soon she would be able to sleep peacefully in their bed.

'I'm beginning to dislike this place,' she said with a shiver, as if a supernatural presence had walked through the deserted dining-room of the run-down hotel, with its sporting prints and odorous bathroom. 'It *never* stops raining.'

The Major looked out of the window at the shrouded mountain in the distance. The rain was part of the charm of the place, and besides, they didn't have the money to go back south as she wanted.

Another dreary afternoon she phoned Somerset from the black box in the hotel lobby.

'Come and stay for a while,' her sister urged her. 'We'll see what can be worked out.'

'What do you mean?' Annabel asked.

'You sound unhappy, darling.'

'It's the weather.'

'I know. I've never liked Scotland.'

Dying rats were crawling all over the house. The Major even found one in the leg of his corduroys hung over the chair. They watched him with outraged eyes as he approached with the poker.

'That's the last of them,' the ratcatcher said, throwing the stinking corpse away.

'How much do I owe you?' the Major asked gratefully.

The ratcatcher was doing a quick mental calculation.

'Twenty pounds, including ferry fare, pilchards, poison.'

The Major paid him cash, then drove to the village to fetch Annabel.

'Are you sure the mice are gone?'

'Every one. And I've got a surprise for you. I've found help.'

He had put an advertisement with a box number in the local paper for a man and wife. She was to do the cooking and cleaning, and he was to help to get the farm going again. The Major had interviewed the couple from the north of the island himself, sitting in the kitchen in his London Scottish kilt of hodden grey cloth which he'd taken to wearing all the time. They told him that they had been looking after a big house for an Englishman who never came to the island, though their wages arrived regularly from a firm of solicitors in Bath. They were both hard workers and had no commitments because their children were grown up on the mainland. His name was Donald, she was Katie, and they were both Christians.

That evening she served roast lamb with potatoes sprinkled with mint in the dinner service that Annabel had had sent up from the south in a packing case.

'What is this?' Annabel asked when the sweet arrived in fluted glasses.

'It's called carraigean, ma'm. It's made from seaweed.'

'From seaweed?' Annabel said, making a face.

'Taste it, darling,' Farquhar urged. He had been served it as a boy on the island.

'It's exquisite,' she said, licking the silver spoon.

It was spring and she began to warm to the place. The crate of days-old chickens arrived from the steamer, and she cupped the yellow balls in her hands, holding them to her cheek before placing them in the run with the wire top that Donald had made for them.

'Will the foxes get them?' she asked anxiously.

'There aren't any foxes on this island, ma'am.'

The Major and Donald went to a sale on the mainland and brought back half a dozen calves on the steamer, the basis of a herd. Donald stripped down the tractor in the barn, then advised his employer that he needed a new one. The Major leafed through the *Scottish Farmer*, for which he had taken out a subscription. Having seen that he couldn't afford a new Fordson, he bought a second-hand one in the north of the island. Donald tried to teach him to plough, but the Major's furrow wasn't true.

When they were having their coffee in the drawing-room the Major could hear the couple talking in Gaelic in the kitchen. He had the instinct that they were talking about himself and Annabel. He felt excluded from the life of the island, and the next day asked Donald if he would teach him Gaelic.

'I'll do that,' Donald agreed.

He taught the Major simple phrases, *how are you? It's a nice day*, patiently correcting his accent.

'Your Gaelic's coming on,' his bank manager complimented the Major.

'I don't know, Archie, it's a damned hard language. I picked up Italian in a matter of months when I was there.'

He hadn't learned it from captured Axis soldiers. One day as he was being driven past a villa in a jeep he had seen a woman walking in the garden, among statues decapitated and maimed by the blasts of the bombardment of Monte Cassino, where the monks yielded, but the stone would not. She was a Countess who had lost her husband earlier in the war, a beautiful woman in a straw hat. The Major had gone visiting, eating olives in the rococo drawing-room with the cracks in the explicit frescos, before they went up to her four poster bed.

stories from an island   61

All her energy seemed to go into their love making, as if the movement of her hips was the best way of forgetting about the ruin of her house and the humiliation of her native land. Within a month the Major could converse in Italian with her. On the day that his unit was pulling out, Cassino broken at last, he took her against the kitchen table, promising her that he would come back after the war.

But he couldn't get the accent right in the Gaelic phrases, and though he studied a textbook in the evenings after Annabel had gone upstairs, the grammar was beyond him.

'You need to persevere, and then it'll suddenly come to you,' Archie Maclean tried to reassure the Major as he put another glass of whisky in front of him.

The Monte Cassino veteran didn't tell Donald that he didn't want any more Gaelic lessons. He simply stopped asking questions.

8.
The Cup of Life

The island ends in the south in a long peninsula (known as 'the Ross') that juts out into the Atlantic. Up until the nineteenth century it had been overcrowded, but the laird had cleared the people across the ocean with the help of the Ainsworthy Line to make way for sheep, and now it was a sad place of very few houses and many ruins in the bracken.

Gille Ruadh spoke of the Ross as if it were another place apart from the island, a place full of quaint, backward people. Very often if he were talking to Archie Maclean about one of them he would lay his cigarette carefully in the ashtray before tapping his forehead.

The MacFadyen brothers lived on the Ross, and the banker did their tax for them. One early summer night her father asked Marsaili if she would like to come with him, for the drive. The banker had obtained his driving licence before the war without having to take a test. When the Austin was lifted off the deck of the steamer his wife wished that it had ended up at the bottom of the sea.

Marsaili went with her father that evening. The road by the sea was single track and the banker had to pull in to allow oncoming vehicles to pass. Coming round a corner, he almost ran into a line of cows crossing the road to be milked, their laden teats close to the tarmac, lowing at his presence as they ambled into the yard. The banker wound down the window and spoke to the farmer in Gaelic.

'He has an overdraft of five thousand, and Head Office are never off the phone to me,' he confided to his daughter when they were on the move again. 'But his people have been in that farm for generations. If I force him to sell the place it'll go to an incomer who'll start to make pottery in the byre for the tourists.'

'That's Colonel Dingwall's place,' the banker pointed out as they passed a substantial house among trees. 'He'll never reverse into a passing place to let a bus come on. He keeps an old copy of *The Times* in the sun visor, and he sits reading it while the bus reverses. That's the kind of people we get on this island, Marsaili, the officer class who think they own the place.'

The cuckoo was calling as they walked across the moor, heather whispering against Marsaili's denims.

'We're going to see three brothers,' her father explained. 'Three men who have never been married and do for themselves in a small house. There is no electricity and I imagine that the sanitation is primitive, so if you need to go, Marsaili, go now.'

As they crossed the moor oystercatchers wheeled crying because they were in the territory of their nests. After two miles there was rock under Marsaili's gym shoes, and a house was in sight at the end of the peninsula.

'The most westerly point on the island,' the banker said, as if it were a geography lesson. 'The next landfall is America, where so many poor souls from this place ended up. No wonder this beautiful island has so many sad Gaelic songs about exile.'

They crossed a narrow headland. The membranes of salmon nets were stretched to dry on tall poles against the sky. The banker knocked the door and a big man had to stoop as he came out.

'This is my daughter Marsaili, Dugald,' Archie said, introducing her in Gaelic.

The clasp of his big hand was gentle. The two other brothers, Donald and Alasdair, were sitting at the supper table. Marsaili was surprised at the tidiness and cleanliness of the place, as if there were a woman about.

'Marsaili, go and have a walk while we talk business,' her father told her.

'Not at all,' Dugald said, signalling to her to remain in the chair. 'If we trust the banker we also trust his daughter.'

They moved the Tilley lamp from the table and the banker took papers out of his pocket. It was time to fill in the tax return. The banker had remarked to his family that the people of the island seemed to believe that they lived in a separate country and therefore didn't have to pay income tax.

'How much did you make at the fishing last year?' he asked.

'Well now, you can tell that from the bankbook here,' Dugald said, producing it from a drawer. He passed it to the banker who did the calculation.

'Three thousand.'

'We had to buy a new net to replace the one that was carried away by a *leumadair*.'

Marsaili looked quizzically at her father.

'The leaper,' he translated. 'It's the word for a dolphin.'

'Aye, he almost capsized our boat, never mind making off with our net,' Dugald said.

'Have you a receipt for the replacement net?' the banker asked.

'Well now, it seems to have got lost. But I can tell you exactly. It was four hundred pounds.'

The banker glanced up and smiled at his daughter as he took down the particulars, and when the papers were filled in he got the three brothers to sign them.

'I don't think you'll have to pay much tax,' he told them.

'That's good,' Dugald said, 'because it's hard making a living from the sea.' Donald made tea and produced a plate of scones.

'They're very tasty,' the banker told them. 'Which one of you is the baker?'

'We take turns,' Alasdair explained and brought the teapot from the grate to fill up Marsaili's cup again.

They conversed in Gaelic. The fishing wasn't what it used to be. A big high-powered boat was coming into the area they leased from the Crown. 'It lays a mile of nets at a time,' Dugald complained. 'No wonder our catches are getting smaller and smaller. If it goes on like this it won't be worth putting the net out.'

'You've earned your retirement,' the banker told them.

'Yes, but when you've worked the sea all your life you would miss it,' Dugald said, and his brothers nodded.

While they were talking Marsaili wandered out of the door and behind the house. There was an noxious smell and she almost stood on the carcass of a seal lying on the rocks, its flippers up. It looked as if its chest had been hacked open with an axe. Whitened bones were strewn about the rocks. She was sickened that anyone could do that to such a beautiful creature for the sake of making as much money as possible out of the salmon netting. What did the three brothers need it for? They didn't have wives, and couldn't run a decent car across the rocky headland.

She wanted to run back across the moor to the car but had to wait for her father. She was retching at the door when Dugald came out and led her into the house.

'What is it, Marsaili?' her father asked.

'It must have been the road down.'

Dugald was looking at his two brothers.

'It was the seal, wasn't it?' he said. 'I'm sorry about that. There's a dead seal on the rocks behind the house,' he explained to the banker.

'Can you not find a way of letting them out of the net?' Marsaili pleaded, not caring that her father was watching her with alarm, because these were valued customers.

'That seal was never near a net,' Dugald said.

'Then why did you kill it?' she confronted them. 'What harm was it doing?'

There was an awkward silence and then Dugald got up. He opened a door and stood aside. An old man was lying in a bed with brass posts, watching the visitors as if he had been listening to the conversation. He lifted a skinny arm and waved to the banker and his daughter.

'This is our brother Hector,' Dugald explained.

'But there are only three of you,' the banker said, bewildered.

'Four,' Dugald corrected him. 'Hector's the eldest.'

The banker went forward to take up his wasted hand. When he spoke in Gaelic he sucked his cheeks into his toothless gums.

'He had an accident when he was a wee boy,' Dugald explained. 'He fell on his head on the rocks behind the house and they took him to Glasgow. They said he was going to die but our father didn't believe them. He wrapped him up in a blanket and carried him home. The old granny was living with us and she told us, there's only one thing that will cure him, a cupful of seal oil three times a week. I've seen it bring grown men back from the edge of the grave, she said.'

Marsaili now understood why the rocks behind the house were a seal cemetery. They must have slaughtered hundreds of the creatures to keep their brother alive. It was as if Dugald were reading her thoughts because he said, 'we've had to go far afield to get seals lately.'

'But why didn't you stop feeding him the oil when you saw he was getting stronger?' the banker wanted to know.

'He's got so used to it that he shouts for it, like a baby,' Dugald explained. He went to a big jug, poured a cupful and held it to the mouth of the old man. He was drinking it audibly as the door closed.

The banker was silent for most of the way home, cutting a corner too fine and almost forcing a Land Rover into the ditch. As soon as they were home he phoned Gille Ruadh at the exchange. 'Marsaili and I were at the MacFadyens tonight,' Archie began. 'We met a fourth brother, Hector.'

There was silence for once at the other end of the line.

'You couldn't have,' Gille Ruadh came back. 'He died when he was a child. It was some kind of accident. They took him to Glasgow but couldn't do anything for him.'

'He's still alive,' the banker assured him. 'I know that what I'm going to tell you won't go any further. He's never had an insurance card, a vote, a visit from a doctor. As far as the state is concerned he doesn't exist. They'll have a job getting him buried.'

'I'm a banker,' Archie reminded his family at supper as they finished the salmon that the MacFadyens had given them. 'That means that people trust me more than the minister, because money's a religion on this island. I should fill in a form for Hector. They'll send a social worker and he'll be taken into the old folks' home and put on a proper diet.'

'You've got to do it, for the sake of the seals,' Marsaili pleaded.

'On the other hand, if he goes into the old folks' home he'll be away from his brothers, and he won't be able to use his Gaelic. He wouldn't last very long,' the banker mused sadly.

He tore up the form. Six months later they heard that Hector had died, peacefully, in his own house on the headland. There was no funeral notice in Black's. As far as the island was concerned, he was long since buried and forgotten. The banker and his daughter went to the interment at the cemetery near the brothers' fishing station. Because women on the island didn't go to graves, Marsaili stayed in the car, watching the three brothers lowering the coffin on the cords, as if they were working a net.

9.
Saskatchewan

It's Games Day. The sun has risen over the bay and is coming through the cotton curtains, laying a golden quilt on Marsaili's bed. She hears her father crossing the landing, then the rasp rasp of his razor as he shaves, humming a Gaelic song. He is Treasurer of the Games and he knows that everything is ready on the field above the town. The marquees that came on the cargo boat have been erected, the latrines dug. He rinses his razor under the tap and his daughter hears the Old Spice, in the flask with the galleon which she gave him for his Christmas, being slapped on. Her mother is now up, going down to the kitchen.

Marsaili goes to the corner of her bedroom and lifts up the two swords. They have authentic looking hilts, but the blades are made of silver painted wood. She crosses them on the carpet and laces up her pumps. Today she is dancing at the Games, and this year she hopes to win the sword dance. She has been practising all winter, making the floor of her bedroom vibrate, with her mother claiming that the ceiling in the sitting-room will come down on top of her as she watches a soap on their temperamental set which sometimes has to be slapped to restore the signal. But her father came up to watch her practising, sitting on the bed as she danced by the window over her dud swords.

'I'll be amazed if you don't win it this year, Marsaili.'

It's Games morning and she is practising, landing on her toes as softly as possible to save them for the competition. Soon her mother will call up that breakfast is ready, but Marsaili will eat nothing more than a brown egg because she has seen competitors in previous years throwing up behind the marquee.

She knows where her father is. He is at the sitting-room window, watching for the dark blue bow of the steamer to slide up to the pier. It left one of the islands in the dawn and is packed with spectators for the Games. Many of them are her father's customers in the bank, but that isn't why he goes down to the pier to wait by the gangway. It's for the pleasure of hearing the Gaelic of another island spoken.

As Marsaili walked along Main Street with her father, with yachts in the bay, he was explaining that the pipe band was coming from the Outer Isles. The Treasurer and the Piermaster agreed that they were most fortunate to be getting such a fine day for the Games. The Piermaster had had a phone call to say that the steamer was full.

'That's strange,' the Treasurer says.

'What is?' his daughter enquires in Gaelic.

'The pipe band usually plays when the boat's coming in.'

There is no music coming across the bay this still morning; only the sound of the steamer's engine, the propeller churning as it eases into the pier. This morning the banker is distracted in his Gaelic greetings to those disembarking. He's watching for the pipe band coming off, but there's no sign of them. When the last person from the island disembarks, his raincoat over his shoulder, his collie at his heels because it too deserves a day out at the Games, the Treasurer goes aboard. His daughter follows.

The pipe band is not in the State Room.

'They must have missed the boat,' the Treasurer says in despair.

Marsaili has gone on below deck to look. She runs back up, shouting to her father to come down. She can see the scene thirty years later. It's as if the entire band has been asphyxiated by fumes from the engine leaking through the bulwark . The drummer is lying with his head on his big drum. The man sprawled beside him has a beatific smile, as though the pipes he's clutching in his arms are a beautiful island woman he's spent the night with.

Marsaili steps over a small drum. She touches the Pipe Major's glittering mace.

'Calum!' her father is shouting, shaking the Pipe Major's shoulder. 'You'll have to get them off. The boat's leaving.'

'We had a few drams after the ceremony, Archie,' he's explaining as he uses his mace to get to his feet, smoothing down his kilt.

The chief had died in exile in America, where he was trying to make a fortune in textiles to buy back his native island. All he had succeeded in purchasing – for an outrageous price – was the ruinous seat of his ancestors. He had managed to put a new roof on when he died of overwork. His body was flown back to Scotland in a bronze casket that took a fork-lift truck to get off the plane. He had left very detailed instructions. A pipe band was to play on the steamer that was taking his cortège out to its last resting place. A lone piper played on the battlements as twelve of the strongest men of the island lowered the casket into the grave that had been dug in the ruins. Then a case of bourbon had been opened.

'We nearly missed the boat,' the Pipe Major is telling the Games Treasurer.

The purser has come down to warn that the boat is leaving in five minutes. Marsaili helps the two men to go round and rouse the band. She carries off two sets of pipes with silver mountings and tassels. The purser has the big drum, but Marsaili has to go back down to search for the sticks to go with it.

At least the band has disembarked. Some of the men are sleeping on their feet.

'I doubt if they'll make it,' the Pipe Major is telling the Treasurer.

Archie Maclean is an inventive man. He has to be, when an irate official from Head Office comes on the phone, demanding to know why he has allowed a customer to overdraw by so much.

Why is he knocking the door of the Ceilidh Hotel? Marsaili wonders. The bolts are drawn for him. Ten minutes later he comes out, carrying a case of lager. He sets it down on the pier and begins handing out the cans of lager to the band. She can hear it gurgling down parched throats. She sees eyes brighten, drums being strapped on, pipe bags being inflated under oxters.

The pipe band has started. Windows are open on Main Street to hear *Hey Johnnie Cope are ye Waukened Yet?*

'It was a clever idea for your father to get us that lager, lassie, otherwise the boys would never have got going,' the Pipe Major with the blue thistles round his hose tells Marsaili.

The band is on the move. The white padded sticks blur in the fists of the man with the big drum. Pipers who seem so tall to Marsaili are fingering their chanters as the band goes along Main Street to the clock, where it will play a medley before the traditional march, led by the chieftain, up to the Games Field. The Pipe Major's hand has a tremble now, but Marsaili will remember this morning when he seems to be throwing his silver mace up at the sun – and catching it as it comes down.

Marsaili is up on the field, her number pinned to her frilled blouse. She has on her pumps and is practising in the subdued coolness of the tent, using her wooden swords. Mothers are fussing round other competitors, straightening the pleats of kilts and exhorting them to dance to the best of their ability.

A girl comes in. She is pretty, with a blue velvet bonnet angled on her blonde hair, and a plaid, held at her shoulder by a cairngorm brooch, trailing at her heels. She is carrying a holdall that says Canadian Pacific, and in her other hand she has two large swords.

'Hi,' she says to the competitors, and comes across to the corner of the tent where Marsaili is exercising to make her toes supple. 'I'm Jeannie Maclean.'

Marsaili goes into her bag to check the programme. There is no such name down for the sword dance. The stranger sees Marsaili looking at her quizzically and says, 'I'm a late entry. Mom posted the form a month ago but it never reached here. I went to see the Treasurer and he says I can compete since I've come such a long way.'

'Where are you from?' Marsaili asks.

'Saskatchewan.'

Immediately that name takes on a romantic resonance because of the way she says it. Marsaili wants her to say it again.

'That's in Canada,' she informs Marsaili, lacing up her pumps. 'One of the prairie states. We have wheat fields that go on for miles.'

Marsaili is trying to imagine the ripe golden crop waving in the breeze when the late competitor adds more information. 'Our people came from this island.'

'From here?' Marsaili queries, surprised.

'U-huh. They were cleared last century and they found their way to Saskatchewan. They did pretty well. We have four combine harvesters on our farm and my father has a herd of Aberdeen Angus he shipped across.' It's not a boast but a factual statement.

'Are these real swords?' Marsaili enquires, reaching across to touch them.

'Claymores. My folks brought them across from this island. My grandfather said we fought with them at Culloden.'

'If they came from here they must have spoken Gaelic,' Marsaili says.

'Sure, but we lost it when we intermarried. My great grand-mother was a squaw. I'd love to learn Gaelic' (she pronounces it Gale-ick). 'Do you speak it?'

Marsaili nods, but she's getting too involved in this conversation instead of preparing for the competition. The Canadian, after all, is a rival, and as she lays the swords on the turf and begins a practice dance, Marsaili sees how good she is. She's dancing as she converses with Marsaili, her shadow turning on the canvas wall of the tent. 'I've been doing this since I was three, first with two wooden spoons on the floor of the kitchen. I need to win today. Mom's outside.'

Marsaili doesn't want to stay in the tent to watch her practise because it's undermining her confidence, so she goes over the hill, past the latrines, already busy with early drinkers, to a quiet hollow where she lays down her swords in the hum of insects and makes her own music with her mouth to dance to. But Marsaili feels there is something lacking. Her feet are heavy and she is aware of the clumsiness of her hands above her head. As she turns her foot touches a blade, and she stops, upset.

Marsaili hears her father's voice through the megaphone, calling the competitors for the sword dance. As she goes back over the hill she feels he has betrayed her by letting the girl from Saskatchewan – she is beginning to hate the name – enter for the competition when the rule says entries in advance. The dancing judges from the mainland are sitting in the shade of a lean-to beside the platform, with paper to mark the competitors on the card tables above their knees. Marsaili sits on the hill to watch, but is not impressed by the standard.

'Number 79, Jeannie Maclean.'

She comes up on to the platform with her swords under her arm and there is a confab among the judges. Yes, she can use her own swords, so long as the steward lays them down. He makes them into a cross for her on the boards. She puts her hands on her hips and bows to the judges as the pipes tune up. Marsaili can see from the first steps what a beautiful dancer she is. She is watching the Canadian's toes and they hardly seem to touch the boards, springing in the air above the blades, now touching a diced stocking. The people around Marsaili on the hillside are enthralled. To her left there is a woman also wearing a Maclean kilt, with a cape. She is standing, holding up her thumbs to her dancing daughter.

Jeannie Maclean is turning in the air, her kilt swirling. She is twenty seconds off the trophy which is waiting on a table in the Secretary's tent. Four nights ago Marsaili watched her father polishing it, and he told her, 'your name will be on this, Marsaili.'

Jeannie Maclean is performing her last movement when she comes down, heavily. Marsaili sees the side of the pump touch the blade which slices through the leather. She is lying on the boards, holding her bleeding foot, and her mother is shouting behind Marsaili instead of going down to her injured daughter.

'You darned fool!'

The Treasurer calls for Dr MacDiarmid through the megaphone and he comes in his Bermuda shorts with his medical bag. Jeannie Maclean is helped off the platform and hops to the first aid tent, her hand on the doctor's shoulder, to have her foot stitched.

It's Marsaili's turn to dance and she turns to bow to the judges in the lean-to. How dearly now does she wish that the trophy for the sword dance was going across the ocean to Canada, to sit in a glass case in a prairie house where Gaelic was once spoken. But Jeannie Maclean is out of the competition. As Marsaili's toes touch the boards she is dancing to the refrain, Saskatchewan Saskatchewan. She sees her father crossing the field, his Treasurer's rosette on his lapel. He has come to watch his daughter and he stands, smiling in encouragement. Marsaili knows she has never danced better because this is a performance for him. Saskatchewan Saskatchewan. She is reaching for the sky. Her mother is on the hillside waving but she has never really been interested in Highland Dancing or Gaelic.

Marsaili can feel her toes so sure, as they come down between the blades. She turns to face the Treasurer, her knuckles on her waist. This is for you, Father, for all the patience and love, for the Gaelic words you give me. She turns to face the marquee. She can see a slumped shadow on the canvas, another shadow hanging over it, an arm raised. This is for you, Jeannie Maclean, with your wounded foot, your treacherous swords and your angry Mom. Marsaili has nothing but pity and love for the wounded Canadian, and as she bows to the judges and the applause rises she knows that one day she will go to Saskatchewan.

10.
The Curam

A blind man could have found his way to MacCallum the baker's shop on Main Street, behind the memorial clock. The people in the flats above left their windows open overnight so that the fragrances from the first batch of bread wakened them.

MacCallum wore a white cap without a brim as he wielded the long wooden shovel at the oven, lifting out the risen loaves. His arms were bare, the tattooed anchors showing that he had been to sea as a young man. In the summer there were queues from the yachts in the bay for his bread when he fired his ovens an hour earlier. MacCallum was one of the few native Gaelic speakers left in the town, and old people went in for the pleasure of his conversation as well as his pastries.

On Saturday night MacCallum got very drunk in the Ceilidh Bar with the steamer engraved on the window. Sometimes he became embroiled in fights, and fists that had pummelled dough into little rolls pulverised the face of a visitor he didn't take to. But on Monday morning he was down at the shop, getting the ovens going, and didn't touch a drop till the next weekend.

Marsaili and her friends were coming home late with heavy baskets and stained mouths from picking brambles on the path to the lighthouse. They balanced their burdens on the stone seats round the clock before going home along Main Street.

'MacCallum's shop's on fire!' Eilidh shouted.

They ran across the street and saw flames coming from the open oven, running down the pole to the floor where MacCallum was lying. The fire brigade broke in his window and carried him out into the night air. He had stayed late to make a wedding cake of rich fruit for a local. It wasn't the smoke that had killed him, but a heart attack.

His widow put the shop up for sale, and everyone had to eat tasteless wrapped bread from the mainland, and cakes with icing like china glaze that came on the ferry. Then Alice Maclean heard in the Co-operative that the bakery had been taken by an English couple.

They came in a tall van with their furniture to a house up the hill. The bakery was renovated. The old ovens that dated from the time before there were any cars on the island were ripped out and new ones fed by gas installed. Because of screens you couldn't see the new baker at work through the window.

Marsaili went in with her mother on the first day of business. There was a lit counter containing all kinds of confections. The bread was in racks above, in strange shapes, dough that had been knotted into figures of eight shapes, elongated into French sticks, slapped into circular crusties dusted with flour.

The new baker was as good as MacCallum, maybe even better because he had a bigger variety. It was said that he had been trained as a pastry chef in a big London hotel. The Quintons were quiet people. They were both in the shop even earlier than MacCallum. While Mrs Quinton washed out the lit counter her husband fired the pristine ovens and slid in the trays of pale dough. But the aromas didn't rise to the open windows above to waken the people. Instead they were ducted away to the back of the shop.

There wasn't any Gaelic spoken in the shop now, and no more fights in the pub because Quinton wasn't a drinker. It was hard to say what he was. He didn't go to any of the three churches in the town, yet he and his wife were never seen on a Sunday. They kept to themselves, and in their house at the top of the town, the curtains stayed shut.

They sold their produce at reasonable prices, and in the evening the lit counter was empty, the racks of loaves cleared. The ovens were scrubbed out, the tiles mopped. The Quintons put up bills for dances and whist drives in their window, but they never went to any functions, not even to the dance held on the pier on Regatta night, when there would be over a hundred yachts in the bay.

One morning Marsaili was in the shop with the basket for the bread order. The boy in front of her was handed a loaf half out of its bag and he swore as he took it.

'What did you say?' Mrs Quinton asked, still holding the other end of the French stick.

'It was hot,' the boy complained.

'You'll go to a place hotter than that oven through there if you use words like that,' Mrs Quinton warned him before she relinquished the loaf.

'I hope you didn't hear the word he used,' Mrs Quinton said as she served Marsaili.

She had heard the word plenty of times, when her friends gathered round the clock in the early evening to try to attract boys, using the sample lipsticks that came taped to the magazines they bought, with advice on their skin and their hearts.

'Are you a believer?' Quinton asked.

Marsaili was so taken aback that she almost dropped the crusty loaf.

'I don't know what you mean.'

'Do you believe in Jesus Christ?' Mrs Quinton enquired.

Marsaili hadn't given the matter much thought. Her parents had made the children go to Sunday school, but the church up the brae was always chilly, and Marsaili's eyes always wandered to the bright day beyond the stained glass windows. But the Maclean clan had rebelled, and there was no more attendance.

Gille Ruadh told them about the history of the town on his nightly visit. There had been five churches at one time, serving a population of five hundred. Gille Ruadh could remember the procession along Main Street on a Sunday morning to the big church with the tower, but the lead had fallen from its windows, and there were crossed planks and a Danger sign at the front door. The Baptist Church further along was only open once a month for half a dozen old people who had to be helped out of cars, and one of them was on a zimmer. Attendance was declining drastically in the other churches.

'I don't go to church,' Marsaili informed Mrs Quinton.

She expected to have the crusty loaf snatched back, but Mrs Quinton leaned over the lit counter of confections and dropped the bread into Marsaili's basket.

'I'm not talking about church-going,' she said. 'You don't have to go to a church to meet Jesus Christ. He's everywhere, even in this shop.'

As she said this she flung her arm dramatically, as if she were dispatching an inferior loaf back to its baker. The screen was open and Mr Quinton was standing in front of the open oven, with its line of little blue jets. He was wearing a tall white hat, and held up the bread pole as if it were a bishop's staff.

'Jesus Christ is everywhere!' he called through to Marsaili in a sing-song voice.

Marsaili was troubled as she left the shop. Her life seemed suddenly to go flat, and she walked home in the shadows of the buildings while her sister and her friends sat in the sun round the clock with young men in blue boots off a yacht that had just dropped anchor in the bay.

'Mr and Mrs Quinton say that Jesus Christ is everywhere,' Marsaili suddenly blurted out over supper.

They were having mackerel, and the banker behaved as if he were choking on a bone.

'Say that again.'

Marsaili said it again, slowly, feeling a strange shiver in her spine.

'I haven't heard that for a long time, not since I was a boy,' her father said. 'There's a word in Gaelic, the *curam*.'

He explained what the word meant over the scattered bones of the mackerel, and the potato skins Marsaili should have eaten to build iron into her body, as Alice said.

The tourists from the steamer had an hour ashore, and they left a lot of money behind.

'It doesn't go into the plates of the churches, that's for certain,' Archie Maclean said.

'Where does it go?' Eilidh asked.

'Into small cars and three piece suites. No wonder Gaelic's declining.'

'Don't get on to that subject again, Archie,' his wife warned him. 'It isn't good for your blood pressure.'

Gille Ruadh had told the story one Saturday evening, after the presentation of the Black Magic. A man had come down the steamer gangway with a black suit buttoned up to his Adam's apple, and a portmanteau bag. He didn't go back on board when the whistle sounded. He was a preacher for an island further north, and his Gaelic was harsh and abrasive.

But once he got into a pulpit, that didn't matter. He had brought the *curam*. The town's drinkers and some of the most disreputable women were falling on their knees on Main Street, stopping the traffic, waving their arms and shouting that they had heard the call of Jesus Christ. The man in the next croft to Gille Ruadh's father was scything one day when the *curam* got him, like a wasp sting. He fell on the scythe blade and almost severed an artery. 'You couldn't get a seat in the biggest church.'

'I don't see what this has to do with the Quintons,' Marsaili said.

'The Quintons have brought the *curam* with them,' Archie explained. 'They've kept quiet until now, but they're trying to push their born-again Christianity. I'm not even sure that it's safe to eat their cakes,' he added, staring at the tempting plate with a straight face. He leaned across and touched Marsaili's nose with his finger. 'Take care you don't get the *curam*, lassie, because you can't get rid of it like lipstick.'

Marsaili began to look forward to going into the bakery, and hung about at the plate glass window till the shop was clear. Mrs Quinton gave her another chapter, waving her hands behind the counter.

'Oh you look the type that will be visited by Jesus Christ,' she told Marsaili. 'He will come anytime, even in the night.'

'Praise be,' her husband said, striking the staff of his oven shovel on the floor.

'How will I know?' Marsaili asked as she took the warm crusty loaf with its many grooves.

'Oh you'll know,' the baker's wife assured her. 'It'll come like lightning, and you'll be filled with a radiance.'

'Like this,' Mr Quinton sang from the back, turning up the blue jets in the oven into hissing flames.

'Come up to the house tonight,' Mrs Quinton whispered across the lit counter.

Even as a mature woman in the city Marsaili can still feel the crunch of the gravel under her shoes as she went up the drive to the secluded house with its closed curtains. Mr Quinton answered the door. He was wearing a Fair Isle pullover, and Marsaili followed him into the big sitting-room where Mrs Quinton was waiting with a plate of their own cakes.

Marsaili started to go up to the Quintons every night while her sister looked for romance at the clock. Marsaili couldn't sleep when she came down from the Quintons. Her room seemed to be filled with a radiance that wasn't from the lamps on Main Street. One very hot night she went downstairs to the bookcase.

'What are you doing?' Eilidh asked, coming into the sitting-room in her trendy pyjamas to sprawl on a chair.

'Reading the Bible,' Marsaili told her.

'What's getting into you?' Eilidh challenged her sister. 'There are some very nice boys staying at the hostel.'

'I've had the call,' Marsaili told her disdainfully.

'Who called you?' Eilidh asked eagerly. 'Is it someone I know?'

'I doubt that,' Marsaili said, and resumed reading Revelations.

Next night when Marsaili came back down the hill her parents were waiting for her in the sitting-room.

'Where have you been?' Alice confronted her

'Up at the Quintons.'

'And is this where you go every night?' her father wanted to know.

Marsaili nodded.

'What do you go up there for?' her mother said in alarm.

'Be calm, Alice,' her husband warned her. 'We need to get at the truth. Marsaili, why do you go to the Quintons?'

'Because they asked me up,' she answered.

'And what do you do when you're up there?' he asked patiently.

'We hold hands.'

'You hold hands?' He sounded alarmed. 'With whom?'

'With Mr and Mrs Quinton. There's nobody else there,' she told her parents.

'And what do you do when you hold hands?' he asked.

'We sing and dance,' she replied.

He was looking at his wife

'Give us an example,' he requested.

'I can't,' she said bashfully. 'We go round and round and sing about being saved by Jesus Christ. Mrs Quinton has a tambourine.'

'And what else?' he asked.

'We watch films,' she told them.

His eyes narrowed.

'What kind of films?'

'Films from America,' she said.

'Oh. . . Archie,' Alice moaned.

'Be quiet, Alice. What kind of films, Marsaili? And when you answer, don't turn your face away.'

'Films of evangelists,' she explained. 'They preach to huge audiences in the Hollywood Bowl. Benny Epps converts hundreds of sinners.'

'And does Mr Quinton do anything else?' her father asked.

'What do you mean?'

'Does he touch you?' he asked, watching his wife again.

'He holds my hand and hugs me.'

'He *hugs* you,' he said, his voice changing. 'Does he kiss you?'

'*No*,' she protested.

'Does he touch you anywhere?'

Marsaili had read about that kind of thing in one of her sister's magazines.

'If you mean does he touch me in private places, he does not,' she said indignantly, looking her father straight in the eye. 'Mr Quinton is not that kind of person.'

'This is big-scale *curam*,' the banker told his wife. 'It's even got into the bread.' He turned to his daughter. 'You are never to go near the Quintons' house again. Is that understood?'

'Are you going to deprive me of the comfort of Jesus Christ?' Marsaili asked him. It didn't sound like her own voice coming from her own mouth.

'Your sister will do the shopping,' Alice said.

'She is the one who betrayed me,' Marsaili said bitterly. 'How many pieces of silver did you give her for lipstick?'

For the rest of that week Marsaili had bad dreams in which someone was beating her over the head with a tambourine and shouting that she would go to hell. She waited outside the baker's until the Quintons locked up.

'I can't come up any more,' she told them.

'Why not?' Mrs Quinton asked.

'My parents forbid it,' she said sadly, looking at her shoes.

'Because we are spreading the word of Jesus Christ,' Mrs Quinton said sadly.

'He could walk on water, but he has never been to this island,' Mr Quinton said.

'When did you first meet Jesus Christ?' Marsaili asked.

'We had a very successful bakery in the south. We used to stay open late, and our teenage daughter cycled home. One night she went under a lorry.' Mrs Quinton's voice had dropped to a whisper. 'I was on tranquillisers, but I couldn't cope. Why our innocent child? I kept asking. What sense was there in God taking her from us in that terrible way? Daniel was drinking heavily and our bakery was shut.'

'A bottle of vodka a day,' Mr Quinton said sadly.

'Our regular customers went elsewhere, and we were almost bankrupt. On the day I was due to go into a mental institution, when I was lying crying my heart out on the sofa, I suddenly felt the spirit of Jesus Christ filling the room, like the fragrance of newly risen bread,' Mrs Quinton revealed. 'I called Daniel through and he sensed it too, didn't you, Daniel?'

Mr Quinton nodded.

'Daniel stopped drinking and I didn't need any more treatment. We came up here to make a new life, and to spread the word about being reborn through Jesus Christ,' Mrs Quinton continued.

'And when we met you, it seemed like a gift from Him, you were so like her,' Mr Quinton added. His eyes were brimming with tears. 'We can't stay here now.'

The Quintons' furniture went away in a tall van. The baker's is now a gift shop, and they keep tartan souvenir dolls in the cold ovens. There are pebbles from Iona in the lit counter. The bread now comes from the mainland, a day old, white and dry in paper.

11.
Doubt

In Archie's film collection his elder son Calum is a shadowy presence. He is seen at the edge of the frame, standing by the sitting-room window, smoking a cigarette, badly in need of a shave after 'a big night,' as his father put it sadly. Alice has a more robust way of putting it. 'We should never have come to this island.'

Calum was clever but lazy at school, a dreamer rather than a scholar. When he should have been doing his homework he was reading other books in advance of his years. By the age of sixteen there was an impressive range of poetry titles in the unstable bookcase in his bedroom, mostly the great moderns. He had poems published in literary magazines when he was seventeen, and his English teacher wrote that he had a 'brilliant creative future ahead of him – provided he disciplines himself.'

Instead of sitting at home studying for his exams, Calum was talking and drinking with Neptune MacIver, the fisherman and his crew, in the public bar of the Arms. At closing time they went along to Neptune's boat, frying kippers on the stove in the cramped galley before getting down to the carry-out of whisky.

Archie is in the tower of the bank house. It's too dark for his cine camera and besides, he doesn't want to record his son lurching along the street from the pier, declaiming poetry to the sea. Alice is raging at his back. 'You should have turned down this place.'

'I couldn't,' her husband protests, still at his look-out post.

'You could have waited till a better place came up. You wanted to come here because of bloody Gaelic. I hate this place. Look what it's done to our son.' (She hears the gate squeaking, and then him falling through the storm doors). 'Isn't it good for Neptune and his kind, telling everyone that they drink with the banker's son?'

Gille Ruadh never mentioned Calum's weakness when he came up, but Archie would receive confidential calls in Gaelic.

'Calum's just put a call to Glasgow through from the Arms. He's in a bad way.'

Archie would have to go along Main Street, to persuade his son to leave his cronies and accompany him home. He even thought of speaking to Dr Murdoch, to see if he could give his son anything to get him off the drink, but Alice said that they would get little sympathy or understanding from that quarter.

Marsaili was very devoted to her brother and tried to point out the hurt he was causing their parents, but though Calum promised to reform, the next weekend he would again be lurching home from the Arms. He and Marsaili had heated arguments about Gaelic.

'Why are you interested in studying that dead language?' he confronted her.

'It's not a dead language. It's the language of our tradition.'

'It's dying out. English is the language of this island. All the great poets write in English. Look at Yeats.'

One evening Calum was sitting in the cocktail lounge of the Arms with a notebook, a whisky and a packet of cigarettes, trying to write a poem when a glass was put down beside his.

'Do you mind if I join you?'

He raised his head to see a good-looking woman with dark hair down to her shoulders. She was already sitting down, holding out her hand.

'I'm Iona MacPhee.'

'Are you here on holiday?' Calum asked nervously.

'If you mean, am I a stranger from the mainland – no. I come from here. I work as a nurse in Glasgow and I'm taking a week home to see my parents. Do you know Dan and Sheila MacPhee?'

'I know them to see,' Calum told her.

'I'm going to buy you a drink,' she announced, opening her handbag.

'No, let me.'

'I asked first.'

She brought him back his whisky, a gin and tonic for herself.

'What are you writing?' she enquired.

'A poem,' he said self-consciously.

'I heard that one of the banker's sons was a bit of a poet. Will you read it to me?'

'It's not finished yet,' he said defensively.

'Maybe I can give you some inspiration,' she said, offering him a cigarette.

The young women Calum knew in the town weren't as sophisticated as this one, with her assured manner, the sliver of lemon in her drink, the turquoise lighter snapped on with the red painted nail to offer him a flame for his trembling cigarette. She told him about her life in Glasgow; the flat she was buying; the ward of the sick and dying; the dances at the Highlanders' Institute she went to on Friday nights. He was waiting to hear about a boyfriend, imagining for this attractive woman – more appealing with every whisky he took – a young doctor in a white coat.

'You'll be going to university,' she said.

He was evasive, saying it depended on how well he did in his examinations.

'I hear you're very clever.'

He coloured at this compliment and bought her another gin. An hour later she asked him to walk her up the brae. This was the first woman that Calum had kissed and he did it awkwardly, against the wall of her parents' cottage.

'Will I see you tomorrow?' she asked. 'We could go for a walk in the evening.'

Several golfers were swinging clubs in the distance as they crossed the hilly course where many balls were driven into the sound below.

'Do you like this place?' she asked him as she accepted a cigarette on the seat turned to the open ocean.

'I find it boring,' he admitted.

'Then why don't you leave – come to Glasgow?' she urged him. 'Go to university and study – make something of yourself, as I had to. If I'd stayed I would have ended up serving in the Co-op. Instead I went to the city and took my exams to become a nurse. It wasn't easy, but I'm glad I did it. There's a satisfaction in coming back here, knowing you've achieved something – and knowing that you can leave.'

When they were passing the road of large villas above the town she took a key from her pocket.

'My mother looks after the Wileys' house. They only come for the summer.'

She unlocked the front door and led him into the spacious hall and up the oak staircase made by local craftsmen. The main bedroom was on the first floor, the bay window overlooking the sound. She removed her clothes, folding them on to the chaise longue. He saw his first naked woman standing by the window, full figured.

She undressed him gently, as if he were a patient brought into her ward. She kissed him and smoothed his brow before she fitted him inside her in a calm unhurried way. He knew he should withdraw, but the experience was too wonderful.

When she came back up she had two glasses and a bottle.

'I'll replace it before I go back to Glasgow,' she told him as she poured two sizeable malt whiskies.

They lay together, drinking and smoking in the antique bed, more like a boat with its carved ends, drapes bound round the elaborate poles with braided cords. It was dark when he went down the brae home.

'Have you been in the Arms again?' Alice confronted him.

'I wasn't in the Arms.'

'The Ceilidh Bar then.'

'I went for a walk across the golf course,' he told his parents.

'Have you got a girl?' his mother asked suspiciously.

'Yes he has,' Marsaili said. 'Who is she, Calum?'

'Someone who'll save him from this place, I sincerely hope,' Alice said. 'Let the rest of them waste their lives and their money in the Arms.'

For the remainder of that week they were up in the Wileys' house, having sex in their bed and drinking their whisky. When Calum went home he sat up late, poems about her pouring from him as he described the firmness of the breasts, the blue eyes of his muse. He felt as if she had made him into a man.

'You know, for the first time I don't want to go back to Glasgow tomorrow,' Iona told him as she passed him the glowing cigarette in the twilight. 'I wish you'd come with me.'

That night he told his parents that he had been thinking about his future and had decided to go to Glasgow University to study English.

'We're so glad,' Archie said. 'But you're too late for this year.'

'I'll go next October. I'll get a job and save some money.'

When they were going to bed that night Alice said to her husband, 'whoever Calum's met seems to be good for him.'

Calum sent away some of the poems he had written to Iona, and they were accepted by a magazine, but he didn't show them to his parents because of the intimate imagery of the firm breasts, the elaborate bed like a barque becalmed above the sound after their lovemaking.

When Iona came home at Christmas they went up to the Wileys' house. The pipes had been drained to stop them from freezing, and the one-bar electric fire couldn't heat the bedroom, a pattern of ice on the window overlooking the bleak sound. She took his hand and put it on her stomach.

'I've brought you a nice Christmas present. I'm expecting.'

He felt a thrill running through his body.

'There's no doubt. I'm a nurse, remember.'

'When is it due?'

'In May. You're going to university in October. You'll need to move down to Glasgow now and then we'll work things out. You'll need to tell your parents tonight. I've told mine. They're delighted. If the banker's son's like his father, he'll stand by you, my father said.'

But after he had seen her to her door he didn't go home. Instead he went down to the Arms and got involved in a big session with Neptune and his crew, who had just brought in a big catch. However, he didn't go along with them to their boat. Instead he got his bearings at the clock for the short but hazardous journey home, lurching up the alley at the side of the bank building.

Alice heard him coming through the storm doors, and Archie went down to help him upstairs.

'I'm going to be a father,' he announced to his family as he stood swaying in the centre of the sitting-room.

'You're drunk,' his mother said contemptuously.

'No, no, she's pregnant. It's due in May. I'm going to get a job in Glasgow before I go to university.'

'Who is *she*?' his mother asked, exasperated.

'Iona.'

'Iona who?'

'Iona MacPhee.'

'My God,' Alice said in despair. 'You haven't got mixed up with that tribe. Marsaili, go to bed.'

She left the room reluctantly, but listened outside the door.

'The MacPhees are tinkers,' Alice told her son. 'Just look at her cheekbones.'

'That's not the point,' her husband said.

'If you hadn't been so keen to come to this bloody place, this wouldn't have happened,' his wife rounded on him. 'How do you know the baby is yours?' she turned to her son.

He swore at her.

When Archie came back into the room he had a glass of whisky.

'Are you mad, giving him that?' his wife protested.

'Sit down, son,' he said, giving him the glass. 'And don't speak to your mother like that. She's worried about you, as I am. I don't care about Iona MacPhee being a tinker, because there's nothing wrong with tinkers. They're perfectly decent people, and anyway, it's years since the MacPhees were on the road. I was speaking to her in the bank the other day, when she was withdrawing money. She's a good looking woman and very polite. But how shall I put this – she bestows her favours.'

It looked as if Calum was going to throw his drink over his father.

'You're talking about the woman I love.'

'I'm a banker, and bankers aren't supposed to divulge what they hear in their office, whether it be about money or not,' Archie continued. 'I'm going to tell you something before you get yourself into a mess. Your lady friend used to work in the Hebridean Hotel before she went to the nursing.'

'I don't know anything about that,' Calum said, shrugging.

'Well I do. There was talk about it at the time.'

'We weren't here then.'

'Gille Ruadh told me,' his father said.

'Why do you believe everything that little moocher says?' Calum said savagely. 'He only comes up here for the free drink you keep pouring him.'

'All my information about your lady friend didn't come from Gille Ruadh, son. I happen to know that every time George Dickson, the manager of the Hebridean, goes down to Glasgow, he stays with her. He told me himself. I won't go into his exact words, but you can take it that Iona MacPhee has a very close relationship with him.'

'So the baby could be his,' Alice came in. 'She's trying to trap you. She knows that George won't leave his wife, but she also knows that the banker's son is a very good catch for a tinker.'

'It's not true,' Calum protested, trying to light a cigarette.

'It's true about George Dickson,' his father assured him. 'We're only trying to save you from getting into a mess.'

They met the next night in the Wileys' house, but he didn't remove his clothes in the big bedroom.

'It won't harm the baby,' Iona explained, stepping out of her skirt. 'I'll go down for a couple of drinks because it's so cold.'

'No,' he said. 'We need to speak.' He went and stood in the window. 'Is it true that George Dickson stays with you when he's in Glasgow?'

'Who told you that?'

'It doesn't matter. Is it true?'

'He has stayed.'

'*Has*? When was the last time?'

'Earlier in the year. But it's only a friendship. I used to work in the Hebridean Hotel before I went away to the nursing.'

'It could be his,' he found the courage to say.

'That's a terrible thing to say. It's yours, and I can prove it from the dates. I thought you loved me. You published these poems to me and I was so proud.'

He looked at her, standing against the light of the window with her firm breasts and high cheekbones. He knew he loved her, but there would always be the doubt.

12.
The Homing Instinct

Marsaili had left her bedroom window open above the bay, but a yacht that had come round the headland in the windless darkness spilled its anchor in the dawn, wakening her. Main Street was deserted. Then she saw a woman in a nightdress feeding a seagull perched on the white railing. Marsaili couldn't hear what was being said but the woman was certainly talking to the bird. She asked her father about it at supper that evening, when they were eating the pail of crabs that the MacFadyen brothers had left behind the storm door.

'That's Mairead,' Archie said, snapping a claw. 'She's got impeccable Gaelic.'

'Are you saying that she talks to the seagull in Gaelic?' Marsaili asked, bewildered.

'Oh no, it wouldn't understand,' her father said.

Marsaili appealed to her mother.

'Your father is being flippant. Now you can see the struggle

I've had over the years to get sense out of him. Mairead is a bit queer. She's been feeding that gull for years.'

'*One* gull?' Marsaili asked. Her parents could be very exasperating.

'I'll ask Gille Ruadh to tell you about her when he's up tonight,' her father promised.

'Mairead? Well, now,' Gille Ruadh said, sliding open a new packet of Gold Flake and taking a sip from the brimming glass that his host had put down for him. 'It was the war that put Mairead queer, though my mother says that there was an uncle who wasn't right. He lived in a croft at the top of the town, and all day long he would sit, watching rabbits.'

'What happened to him?' the banker asked, trying to keep a straight face at this latest example of insular eccentricity.

'He was sent to the asylum. I was here in the early part of the war, before I was called up.'

Gille Ruadh recreated the town. The prime harbour had become a naval base, and the population went from three hundred to a thousand. There was a floating dock to repair ships. Every Sunday the WRNS were marched up the back brae to church like a platoon of nuns.

'They were very strictly watched,' the narrator told his audience.

'No romancing?' Archie prompted.

'Well – a little,' Gille Ruadh said coyly, looking at his foot. 'It was a strange time. Everyone was keyed up with all the coming and going. I would be coming down the brae when a flying boat would land in the bay, skimming along as if it was going to end up in the garden of the Masonic Lodge. The Arms was accused of selling hooch,' he explained. 'It made the sailors mad. Instead of wanting to fight the Germans they wanted to fight their own officers. That's the kind of place this was.'

'You were going to tell us about Mairead,' his host reminded him.

stories from an island   97

'Before the war she did the books in Black's. I think she got bored with serving nails and paint, so she went to work in the NAAFI in the evenings. I was in the hall the night the first fox-trot was called. It was a dance none of us had heard about. We were all used to doing eightsome reels and jigs. But a flying boat pilot called Charlie Morgan got up and went across the floor for a partner. He choose Mairead.'

After another swallow of whisky Gille Ruadh described the nifty footwork of the aviator as he steered Mairead round the floor. She was a well-built young woman with auburn hair, and they made an attractive couple as they went round. Soon other couples got the knack and in no time at all the floor was crowded as the town danced to a record of Benny Goodman through a fluted horn.

'I'm making it sound like an endless party,' Gille Ruadh said. 'But there was a sad side to it. Locals wanted to be polite to the English incomers, the sailors and airmen, so they stopped speaking Gaelic.'

Marsaili reminded their visitor that they had left Mairead doing the fox-trot in the arms of the flying boat pilot.

'He was a very handsome man. He used to land his plane and then walk out on a float, waving to Mairead. Did I say that he was Welsh?'

'No you didn't.'

A lot of the girls in the town were very envious of Mairead. Who else had a boyfriend who flew over their house, though he got into trouble with the base commander?

Gille Ruadh and others learnt to fox-trot, but nothing like Mairead and Charlie. They could have picked up prizes in peacetime for their fox-trots. And tangos. 'Mairead was a beautiful dancer,' he added, shaking his head in fond recollection.

The life of the town went on. The people could see the convoys passing down the sound, and one afternoon a damaged submarine came in, its stern gun going up and down. It turned out that Archie

MacNab was in the crew, and that he was trying to signal to his parents to put the kettle on. Boats and planes came and went. And there were bodies. Gille Ruadh recalled the night the ship in the convoy was hit by a stray plane at the entrance to the sound. There must have been fifty bodies in the bay by the morning.

'They laid them out in rows in the Masonic Lodge, the poor souls. MacTaggart the joiner couldn't make that number of coffins, so they brought them in a landing-craft from the mainland. They're buried up in the cemetery.'

Gille Ruadh described another tragedy. The distillery was used as a magazine, and one afternoon a blast broke most of the windows in Main Street and left six personnel dead, as well as extensive damage to the distillery. The rumour went round that a German spy had sabotaged the magazine, but Gille Ruadh said that it was a tragic accident.

'What about the Welshman?' Archie persisted for his daughter's sake.

He had a beautiful tenor voice and started singing with Mairead in the Gaelic choir. He seemed to have settled in the town. People kept boats in the bay and he kept a seaplane. He left in the morning to look for U-boats because they were lethal for the convoys.

Did the lone Celtic aviator sing Welsh songs to himself as he cruised the clouds? Marsaili wondered.

'He came back before dark and had his supper in the NAAFI,' Gille Ruadh continued. 'Then the tables were cleared, they put a record on the turntable and they did the fox-trot. After I was finished work on the telephone exchange I would go up for a dance, but we were very busy, with so many calls, and you had to be careful. If you gave anything away a German plane could have come into the bay and done an awful lot of damage.'

'You were talking about Mairead,' Marsaili reminded him.

'She and Charlie announced one night after the Gaelic choir that they were going to get married. You could always get a case of whisky from big Norman in the Ceilidh Bar. It was some night. We ended up in the NAAFI where – well, I won't go into that.'

The banns were called, and Mairead was working on the dress. It was actually a silk parachute. The story went that Morgan had bought it for a few pounds on the black market. Others said that it was his own and that he risked court martial and his own life by using it for that purpose. Gille Ruadh was out for a walk with the dog when the pilot and Mairead appeared on the golf course. It was a day with no wind and they spread the parachute out on the first green and cut off enough material to make a wedding dress. They gave the cords to the scout hall for their tents.

Marsaili could picture the auburn-haired beauty coming out of the church on the hill in her billowing dress of parachute silk, as if she were going to take off over the bay where the groom's seaplane was riding at anchor. Did they fly off to some remote Hebridean island for their honeymoon?

'There was no wedding,' Gille Ruadh said.

'He jilted her,' the banker said sadly. 'A lot of hearts were broken in wartime.'

'It would have been better if he had,' Gille Ruadh said enigmatically.

It was a choppy day and there was some doubt about the planes flying. Gille Ruadh was watching from the exchange window, having a smoke between calls. The Welshman with the glorious voice made it up into the sky, heading west, shadowing another convoy. He didn't come back at six, though Mairead was waiting in the NAAFI with a bowl of broth for him.

'She came to the exchange that night,' Gille Ruadh reminisced. 'Did we know anything about a missing flying boat? Even if we had, we daren't have said.'

Mairead was distraught. She stayed on the seafront for most of the night as if a flying boat could land in a strongly westerly without a moon. She took a fever and Dr Murdoch said it had affected her brain, because she became a different person. When someone asked for a pound of nails in Black's she would keep pouring them into the pan on the scales, as if she had forgotten how to use the brass weights.

'So she's queer. That's why she talks to the gull,' Marsaili said. You're spoiling John's story,' her father rebuked her.

Gille Ruadh had been called up because being hall porter in the Hebridean Hotel was not a reserved occupation, even though the navy had requisitioned it for officers. After a period of training in the south he was sent out to North Africa. He was home on leave after his exertions at Tobruk when his mother took a call from Mairead.

'The Welshman's back,' Mrs MacDougall told her son.

He can't be back, Gille Ruadh insisted. His flying boat was lost.

'Mairead says he's back, and that they're going to get married,' Mrs MacDougall went on.

Gille Ruadh began to wonder if the Welsh aviator had run into bad weather and flown his flying boat to another base.

'Then why didn't he get in touch with her, when they were going to get married?' Marsaili challenged their visitor.

'The ways of the human heart are strange, Marsaili, as you will no doubt discover in the course of your life,' her father remarked. 'Go on with your story, John.'

'I met Mairead down the town that afternoon. I expect Charlie will lead you off with the fox-trot at the wedding dance, I said to her.'

'Come and see him tonight,' Mairead said. 'He's asking for you. You were very good to him with whisky when it couldn't be got.'

Gille Ruadh duly went down and Mairead came across the road. 'Where is Charlie?' he asked. 'There,' she said. 'Standing behind you.' Gille Ruadh turned round. He was looking for the Welshman on the deck of one of the boats in the bay, but all he could see was a herring gull on the rail, squawking at him. 'Charlie's plane went into the sea but he came winging back to me,' Mairead said. 'Here, Charlie.' She put her hand into the carrier bag and held a hunk of bread in her fist for him to peck on.

'What did you say to her?' Archie asked the narrator.

'What could I say? That's no airman. That's a herring gull and we have dozens of them on our roof every morning screaming and scattering the rubbish from the bins. I couldn't possibly say that. So I said, welcome back, Charlie, and the bird squawked.'

'Mairead is still feeding her fiancé,' the banker said. 'He still comes back to her morning and evening. It's very touching.'

'How long has he been coming?' Marsaili asked.

'Over twenty years,' Gille Ruadh calculated.

'But it *can't* be the same gull,' she pointed out.

'I don't know much about the life cycle of the herring gull,' her father said. 'What does it matter so long as Mairead's happy?'

A week after this conversation, Marsaili went along the street to where Mairead was feeding the gull on the rail.

'You're the banker's daughter,' she said. 'You're very like your mother.'

'Gille Ruadh was telling us that Charlie came back,' Marsaili said to her in Gaelic.

Her face lit up.

'Oh it's so good to hear Gaelic again. This is Charlie.' She rummaged in the bag and produced the bread.

Marsaili got into the habit of going along to meet Charlie most nights, and she and Mairead had long conversations in Gaelic while the gull squawked at their backs.

'Where has he been all day?' Marsaili asked, so sorry for the elderly woman in her delusion.

'Out at sea,' she said, lowering her voice and giving Marsaili an enigmatic look.

Charlie disappeared later that summer. Marsaili wondered if he had died of old age out in the ocean. She could still see Mairead down at the railing with her carrier bag, her wispy hair blowing in the wind as she watched the west. Then she had a stroke. They found her lying on her kitchen floor in her nightdress, clutching a carrier bag of stale bread, with the window open on the bay and the curtain being blown in. The banker was her executor. She left her money to the Airmen's Benevolent Fund.

13.
Counterfeit

Marsaili was wakened by the rumble of an anchor chain. When she went to her window she saw that a barge had come in overnight and was moored off the pier. In mid morning her father came up from the bank to tell her that new treasure hunters had arrived. That evening, when Gille Ruadh came down the brae, the banker's first question to him was (having set down the prompt of a brimming dram), 'so Colonel Fawcett didn't find the treasure, John?'

For Marsaili's benefit Gille Ruadh resumed the story from where he had left it, Miss Staples posing on the barge in a sailor suit and jaunty nautical cap in the summer of 1928, holding the coin that Colonel Fawcett – her employer or lover, probably both – swore was a Spanish ducat, but which, Gille Ruadh had insisted, was of much more recent origin and had come from the waistcoat pocket of Dodie MacFarlane.

The dealer in Spink of London didn't even screw his jeweller's glass into his eye to pronounce on the authenticity of the coin. Instead he used his thumb nail to scrape away the paint that Dodie had first used to gild a picture frame for his mother, having put a penny on the kitchen range and pounded it with a hammer to give it an antique look.

Colonel Fawcett pocketed the fake ducat and gave more interviews to newspapers, explaining that investors from all over the globe were putting money into his Man o' War syndicate, and that he was making a deadline of midnight in two days' time for the prospectus to close. That evening abuse was being shouted from New York at Mrs MacDougall through her headphones at the exchange, a Yank insisting on being put through to Colonel Fawcett so that he could invest his ten thousand dollars before midnight. The man was yelling that he knew the King and would get her dismissed from her post if she didn't connect him, but the operator yanked out the plug and went to eat her frugal supper, complaining in Gaelic to her son that the world was full of gullible fools.

During the rest of that summer Colonel Fawcett squandered forty thousand pounds of new investment, riddling sand and barnacle shells from the bed of the bay. His divers brought up encrusted cannon balls, and pieces of china. No more gold coins. Nothing of value. Miss Staples and he continued to share interconnecting rooms in the Hebridean Hotel where, as Gille Ruadh told the banker and his daughter, the management were getting worried by the size of the outstanding bill.

'Why didn't they put him out?' Archie Maclean wanted to know. 'He was obviously a shyster.'

Ah, but a clever shyster who claimed to have made millions out of pearl fishing in Ceylon, a claim that could not be corroborated in the Hebrides. He had a wardrobe of made-to-measure plus-four suits, mostly in flamboyant checks, with matching caps, and he had the accent of a gentleman, if not the habits, because the French letters continued to be pressed under the mattress, like small pink flowers, and Miss Staples, secretary or kept woman, continued to tuck her enticing curls under the brims of her comely cloche hats before she went out to the barge, where she sat on the other side of the grille from the Colonel, watching the dancing debris from the depth. There was no glint of gold in the autumn sun, except from a curl that had come down from under the cute felt brim.

The gales arrived, and the barge dragged at its moorings. It was too dangerous to send divers down into the sea that came tumbling in from the sound. Under such leaden skies, gold would not be recognised on the grille. So the trunks of the Colonel and Miss Staples were packed and taken down the brae on a lorry this time, rather than risk the heart of another horse. The steam derrick swung the trunks on to the deck of the *Lochspelvie*, where they were lashed under tarpaulins. The barge had already gone, and in the Ceilidh Bar Dodie MacFarlane cursed the shyster, who had handed him his last month's wages in an envelope before boarding the steamer. The gangway had gone by the time that Dodie had tipped out the contents on to his palm – the penny that he had pounded and gilded.

'So what happened to the Colonel and his paramour, John?' the banker wanted to know.

This was one of the few questions Gille Ruadh couldn't answer, though he and his mother continued to intercept all calls to the island. Colonel Fawcett could have gone back out to Ceylon, to bring up priceless pearls from the deep – or rather, have underpaid natives risk their lives and lungs in bringing them up for him. Perhaps he had married Miss Staples, and they were living on credit in a fine house with servants in the Home Counties. Or perhaps he was languishing in prison on some continent, having been caught out in another scam.

The new search for the treasure had nothing to do with the Man o' War Syndicate. The Duke, who owned the salvage rights, was supervising the operation himself, having suggested to the navy that raising a Spanish galleon from a bay in the Western Isles was a good training exercise.

From her high window Marsaili watched His Grace's kilted figure on the barge, examining the vibrating belt of material that the huge hose had sucked up. She watched the divers in their tight black wet-suits, with golden zigzags on their thighs, like gorgeous creatures from the deep, flipping over the sides of the barge to show the Duke their latest find – an intact plate made of pewter. Dodie MacFarlane was not part of the local crew, having trodden on a mine in the Western Desert.

In the evenings, when it became too dark to dive, the navy men came ashore, to drink in the Ceilidh Bar with the locals. Some of them made assignations with females of the town, displaying the same litheness behind the pier as they used out in the bay.

Marsaili also saw newspaper men, resting their telephoto lenses on the railings, or interviewing the Duke on the barge. She read the words she hadn't been able to hear in the next day's paper. Yes, His Grace was confident that they would find the treasure before the end of the summer.

In August, when Marsaili went to the Regatta dance on the pier, a naval rating in a white topped cap shining in the moonlight asked her up for a waltz. As they went round the bollards to Alasdair MacTavish's music he told her his name was Alfred. He was eighteen years old and hailed from Portsmouth. His father had been in the navy before him, and his grandfather had served under Admiral Beattie.

This was not the first person to kiss Marsaili Maclean. That had happened the previous year, after a school dance, with a boy called Hamish Low, who was in competition with her for the Dux Medal. The naval rating pushed back his white-topped hat to engage with her, but as they walked down the path to the lighthouse Marsaili found even more thrilling his account of his dives in the bay.

What like was it, down there? Dark, dangerous. The suction pump of the barge disturbed the floor of the bay, which was scattered with centuries of debris. From the Spanish galleon? No, from rubbish that the locals had thrown into the bay; bottles that galley staff had tipped out through the portholes of steamers. They had even found a plate from the *Comet*, the first commercially successful steamboat, and this had gone to the museum in Glasgow.

Marsaili dreamed that she was swimming beside her naval escort down in the depths of the bay, her hand in his, blindly groping the bottom in the search for a chest that had long since spilled out its golden bullion.

One night he brought her a souvenir under his jacket.

'What is it?' she asked, as she handled it on the dark path below the Hebridean Hotel, where Colonel Fawcett and Miss Staples had had interconnecting rooms.

'Guess.'

'I can't.'

'It's a skull.'

Marsaili nearly dropped it. 'Why did you bring it up?' she asked, terrified.

'Because the Duke asked us to bring everything up.'

'Has he seen it?' she wanted to know.

'No, but he will by the morning – unless you want it.'

'Put it back where you found it,' Marsaili pleaded.

'It would only get sucked up and smashed.' He took the cigarette from his mouth and put it inside the skull, making the eye sockets glow, like a turnip lantern.

Next morning, His Grace showed the skull to the world's press. It was small, and an archaeologist who was on the barge to give guidance speculated that it was the skull of a cabin boy who might have served the Master of the vessel himself before they were both sent to the bottom by the treacherous explosion.

The skull appeared in the papers the next day. That evening, when Gille Ruadh came down, he was highly critical.

'My mother says they shouldn't have brought up the skull. Bad luck comes to those who disturb the dead, she says. When Seumas

Ban ploughed up bones on his croft he was dead within the week, yet never had so much as an ache in all his years.'

Marsaili couldn't sleep that night because of her terror at having handled the skull. She began to have pains in her head and wondered if she would make the morning. At about 2am she called out for her mother, but Alice said they were period pains.

'They're not due till next week,' her daughter told her.

Marsaili was no longer meeting her rating from Portsmouth. He had become a sinister figure to her, the bearer of death from the deep, and she was frightened to kiss him now, in case he transferred something to her from the skull, some mysterious illness that would paralyse her, if not kill her. Now the black wet-suited divers on the barge beyond her window had become scavengers, sinister as cormorants perched on the sides of the barge. As for the Duke, he smoked through a long bone holder as he watched the vibrating grille for the glimmer of gold that would redeem his estates.

At the end of the summer, the artefacts that had been collected were laid out on the floor of the hall for the locals to inspect. Marsaili walked past the cairn of encrusted cannon balls, the fragments of pottery, a boot that could as easily be Victorian as Elizabethan, perhaps lost when a boy was carried kicking aboard one of the Ainsworthy Line's emigrant ships.

But where was the skull? Not among the debris at her tennis shoes. The Duke must have taken it with him, to his castle on the mainland, an added attraction for the tourists.

As usual, Gille Ruadh had the answer. His Grace hadn't taken the skull. In fact, he didn't want anything more to do with the skull. The day after he had handled it, a signet ring that had graced the little finger of five generations of dukes had fallen off and plopped into the bay.

'The skull's up in the Hebridean Hotel,' Gille Ruadh told the Macleans in the bank house.

Mr Forsyth the proprietor had taken it off the Duke's hands. He put it on a ledge in the cocktail bar, as an attraction. Guests from the mainland, and visiting yachtspeople having drinks before their seafood dinner, asked for the skull to be lifted down. They sat it on the bar counter and pretended to talk to it. One visitor, with a gift for ventriloquism, even made it speak in pidgin Gaelic.

Then one night it disappeared. The proprietor threatened to have the constable search all eighty yachts in the bay. Next morning, after the departure of one particularly riotous crew who had spent the previous evening drinking the Hebridean Hotel dry of malt whisky, the skull was found on the doorstep by a housemaid.

When the proprietor drilled holes in the skull to affix it for safety to the wall, he developed excruciating headaches in precisely the places where his drill had bit in. All kinds of things started to go wrong in the premises. The water tank ruptured in the attic, bringing down four ceilings over two floors, including the suite occupied by Colonel Fawcett and Miss Staples. One of the maids, hoovering the bar where the skull hung, broke her leg when she tripped over the machine's cable.

The newspapers now ran stories about the 'curse of the skull'. A Minister came from Morayshire, to exorcise the spirit within the skull, using a special prayer. On his way back to the mainland he had a heart attack on the steamer, dying before it reached the mainland.

As the autumn gales whipped up the bay Marsaili began to miss the naval rating who had spent the summer flitting among the fish. At his castle the Duke was flabbergasted to get a bill for thirty thousand pounds from the Admiralty, 'for the use of our manpower and machines in trying to recover artefacts from the Spanish galleon allegedly wrecked in your bay,' the clerk had written in copperplate.

On a Sunday morning Marsaili noticed a procession coming along Main Street, with something resting on a cushion. The banker took his cine camera into the turret window to record the historic ceremony. The local minister went down the steps in his vestments, stepping aboard the launch, the skull wobbling on the cushion. His elders went with him, and they were followed by a flotilla of boats which made a circle round the place where the Spanish galleon was reputed to have gone done. The Reverend Thomson said a short prayer, and then, holding up the cushion dramatically, after the singing of *Will Your Anchor Hold?* to a melodeon, he tipped the skull back into the depths.

When the banker's exclusive film of the ceremony came back from the mainland the box was marked: 'Spoilt by overexposure.'

14.
Housebound

Because of the cliffs, the harbour at the end of the mile-long promontory could only be reached from the sea. The Vikings had used it as a raiding base, cutting slipways into the rock for their galleys and leaving behind a harsh name. A thousand years later these slipways were still in use by the MacKinnons, the owners of the solitary house. No one on the island knew how long the family had lived there, but it was certainly outwith living memory.

The single-storey house originally had had a heather roof, but the Atlantic storms had kept carrying it away, so it had been replaced with slates. There was no possibility of bringing an electric cable along the headland, and the MacKinnons didn't have an engine. All the cooking was done on a range which had been brought in by boat sixty years before. It was fired by peat which the two brothers cut on the island, bringing it round by boat and tossing the sods to their sister, who stacked them against the side of the house. She was dressed the same as her twin brothers, in blue dungarees and wellingtons, and her hair was tied back with a piece of rope. Despite her appearance, she was a good-looking woman, with high cheekbones and a determined mouth.

Cailean MacKinnon had taken his three children to school in the launch, and collected them in the evening. If the weather was too bad, they didn't go. He drowned when the two boys were twelve. It was a freak accident, a wave for which they had a special Gaelic word coming at his back and pushing him overboard. The brothers took their sister to school.

On the day they were fifteen they stopped going, and so did Flora. The teacher had sent a note to their mother to say that she was clever, and should be given 'her chance', but Annie MacKinnon couldn't read English. She couldn't even speak it. Her only language had always been Gaelic, which she could neither read nor write. The family used nothing but Gaelic at home, and on the sea, when the twins were fishing.

The family had held the salmon netting rights round the headland for over a hundred years. There was no competition for the lease from the Crown, even though the rent was peppercorn, because the coast was too treacherous, with hidden reefs that could rip the bottom off a boat. The twins laid their glittering catches in boxes, which they nailed up and took round in the launch to the pier, for shipment to the south. When the cheques came back in payment they took them round in the boat to the town, when they went once a month for their provisions.

Standing at the ornate window of his bank office, Archie Maclean would see the boat coming curving into the bay, with the three of them aboard. He had sufficient view to watch them tying up at the stone pier and coming along the street in their dark oilskins and seaboots which the woman in the middle also wore, with a souwester. The three of them go into the shop for their groceries. Flora has the list in her head. They never buy any meat, because they keep sheep on the headland and butcher one from time to time. They never buy the bread that comes in oily wrapping, already sliced, from the south, because she bakes their own. They buy a sack of flour, a special order which Alasdair lifts on to his back to take down to the boat.

Flora is looking at the tins on the shelves. She would love to ask for a small tin of peaches, because she tasted them years before, at a school treat. She remembers their rosy yellowness, and how she spooned up the syrup. But her brothers wouldn't allow her to buy peaches because they never have sweet things. If she wants biscuits, she can bake them in the temperamental black oven that is cool on days when the wind is from the north.

The month's supply of pipe tobacco is stacked in tins on the counter. They buy a bottle of whisky, but this is strictly for medicinal purposes, for a toddy if one of them has a cold. The boxes of provisions are carried down on to the boat, and they go back along Main Street again for a barrel of paraffin which they kick along the street to the pier, bouncing it down the steps to the boat, where it is roped to a seat.

The MacKinnons then went along to the bank, and asked to speak with the manager. Archie Maclean shook hands with the three of them, noting that the woman's grip was as strong as a man's, and that she was also attractive, 'if she would clean herself up', the phrase he would later use to his wife when describing this visitation.

Alasdair took a pocket-book from inside his oilskins. He opened it and laid a wad of cheques on the manager's desk. These were from the fish merchants they dealt with, and Archie Maclean sat listing the totals, then adding them up.

'Nine hundred pounds.'

The other twin nodded, as if he would never doubt his banker's calculation.

'Put that in the account,' Alasdair instructed.

'Do you need any cash?' Archie asked. He always asked this question and always received a negative answer. He had realized long ago that the MacKinnons were selling part of their catch for cash and using the money for living expenses. Which meant that they weren't paying tax on it.

'Would you like some tea?'

The tray with the scones was waiting for him upstairs. The three visitors pulled chairs round the desk and conversed with their bank manager in Gaelic as they ate and drank. Archie kept noticing the way the sister was watching him from under long lashes. She was very dark looking, and he recalled the story that some of the crew from the Spanish Armada galleon had got ashore and copulated with the local women before being rounded and taken to Edinburgh. This woman said nothing as she nibbled at her scone.

All the talking was done by her two bothers, and they were recalling that day after the war when a land mine had come bobbing ashore.

'We put a rope round its horns and towed it round the headland, where we tied it to the rocks,' Alasdair recalled. 'Then we went for the coastguard.'

'You could have been blown up,' the banker said, thrilled by the descriptive Gaelic as much as by the drama.

'Well, we didn't want it to make a mess of our slipway.'

They finished their tea, shook hands and went away. Archie watched them walking along Main Street, with the sister in the middle. They looked a sinister bodyguard in their long boots and flapping oilskins. Why did she stay out in that lonely place with these two men, who communicated with the sea far easier than they did with their fellow creatures?

The provisions were unloaded and she returned to her chores, using the oven when the wind wasn't against her. They returned to casting their nets, sitting at their supper with their seaboots hanging from their waists, like heavy rubber skirts, talking in Gaelic about the sea, as if it were a temperamental woman. They had many Gaelic words for its treachery, for the blows it could deal you when your back was turned to it.

They nailed their catches in dripping boxes, amassing in the bank a sum of money that they would never spend, because their only extravagance was the boat and the nets. They would never exchange the boat, and the three of them mended the nets carefully, sitting on the shore, working their flawless Gaelic into the membrane under the towering volcanic terraces.

She was sick of the sound of the sea, sick to death of eating salmon and mutton. Sick, too, of Gaelic. She was planning this other life, waiting for her opportunity. It came one afternoon when a strange boat came into the bay. It was a yacht that had run out of water, and she allowed the two men in blue oilskins to fill their plastic container at the outside tap.

'Where are you going?' she asked in uncertain English.

They told her that they had been cruising among the Western Isles for a week and were now returning to the mainland.

'Can you give me a lift?' she asked.

They waited until she emerged with the brown suitcase with metal at the corners that one of the brothers had bought when he had had to go to hospital for an essential operation years before.

She sat on the deck of the boat, the breeze filling the sails above her. The man at the helm had a chart spread out before him as he negotiated the treacherous reefs her brothers knew so well. When they had anchored in the busy bay they took her ashore in their rubber roundabout. She had never been to the mainland before and was surprised at the size of the town.

She had brought a hundred pounds in cash with her from the tin on the mantelpiece. The first night of her freedom she stayed in a bed and breakfast on the seafront, with a woman who spoke

Gaelic and who questioned her closely on where she came from.

'I don't recognise the dialect.'

Flora had always been taught never to give anything away at school about her home circumstances, though some of the girls in the playground had called after her that her family were squatters. So she avoided the question and told the woman that she was looking for work.

'What kind of work?'

'As a waitress.'

'Well, the Isles View Hotel is always looking for staff. Mind you, they work you very hard. If you're going for an interview I would advise you to change into something more suitable. I can lend you a dress.'

Another rule was that the MacKinnons never took anything from anybody for nothing – except the interest that accumulated in their account in Archie Maclean's bank. So Flora went and bought the cheapest dress, with a subdued print, at the chainstore shop that had a branch in the town.

'What experience have you had of dining-room service?' the smartly dressed manager of the Isles View asked this dowdy creature in the ill-fitting dress, with shoes that seemed to belong on a much older woman.

'I worked in an hotel before,' Flora lied, desperate for a job.

'Silver service?'

She nodded, though she didn't know what the phrase meant. She was taken up to a room under the slates she would share with three other maids. When she tied the apron round her hips and went downstairs to the dining-room she was lost. The only table she had set at home was a basic one, a knife and fork at each place. She stood watching as the other girls laid out the sweet knife and fork alongside.

The bus tour were in their seats even before the reverberations of the gong had ceased. Flora laid before them the lukewarm plates of packet soup, and brought the extra slices of bread that they demanded. The head waitress gave her a ticking off, telling her that they were only allowed one slice of bread per person.

The heat in the plates didn't bother Flora, because she had been used to lifting out tins of bread from the temperamental oven at home. But while she was serving the steak pie and vegetables she tripped and tipped the meal into a lap. The stout woman was on her feet, raging that this was the only clean dress that she had with her. The head waitress had to come across, to apologise and promise that the hotel would get it cleaned, express, at their expense.

The dinner was even more complicated, because some of them ordered wine, and Flora poured it over the cloth instead of into the glass.

'You haven't done any waitressing before,' the head waitress confronted her when the guests had departed to watch a Highland show in the lounge.

'I need the job,' Flora pleaded.

The head waitress took pity on her and gave her a lesson on laying out cutlery and serving wine. Flora began to feel more confident. In the evening, after she had finished work, she would walk up the hill and sit on a bench, looking across to the mountains of her island. In the first few days she felt homesick for the harbour with its incisions in the rock, and for her dour brothers, but now there was a sense of liberation, of joy. One night she went out with the girls to a dance, and found that she had a sense of rhythm.

The wine waiter from another hotel asked to walk her home. His name was Aldo and he told her that he came from an island called Sicily where the heat was intense. She let him kiss her in a doorway. It was a tender moment and they arranged to go to the cinema.

She had her hair styled and bought new clothes from her first month's wages. If they were both off on a Friday evening she and

Aldo went to the dancing. He taught her to waltz, his hand on her spine.

He was teaching her some words of Italian, and in return she taught him how to say good morning and good night in Gaelic, and also to say, 'it's raining,' because he was always complaining about the weather.

'How do you say my love in Gaelic?' he asked.

She hesitated. *'Mo ghaol.'*

She had to pronounce it several times before he got it right.

'I take you to Sicily with me,' he promised.

'Mo gul,' he repeated, looking into her eyes.

One evening, a man from the tour was flirting with her as she put the salmon salad in front of him. She was bringing him the horseradish sauce when she felt a strong pair of arms encircling her from behind. She was screaming and kicking as her brother in his seaboots carried her out of the dining-room, among the stunned tables, down the steps and across the esplanade to the slipway where the other brother was waiting with the launch. The people from the tour were crowding the windows to watch as the launch roared away with the struggling woman in the bottom.

15.
The Gay Gordons

Marsaili was home for a holiday and was walking along the seafront in the autumn night when she heard an accordion. Alasdair MacTavish was playing in the lounge bar of the Ceilidh Hotel. It was the Gay Gordons, and as Marsaili stood listening she thought about Bobby Lamont. She was in the warm infants' room in the school up the brae, crowding at the windows with the others. They were mocking Bobby, who was limping around the playground in the rain, looking for the shoe the boys had pulled off him. There was a hole in his sock and he was crying.

From the first day he arrived, his new satchel on his back, Bobby was bullied, and Miss MacColl shouted at him in the classroom because he couldn't do basic sums. One afternoon the boys dragged Bobby into the porch and tried to remove his trousers. He put up a ferocious fight, and when Marsaili found him he was lying on the concrete floor, his knee gashed. She ran for Miss MacColl, and the teacher brought her first aid box and used iodine.

It's Christmas time, and the hall is decorated with paper chains for the party. Clusters of balloons hang from the rafters. Bobby comes in with his mother. He is wearing a little kilt that must be a cut-down of his mother's, because it is buckled the wrong way. Miss MacColl announces the Dashing White Sergeant, and shows the class how to do the dance. Alasdair MacTavish plays his accordion, his shoe keeping time on the platform. Marsaili is holding Bobby's hand, and when he faces her, his fists on his hips, he begins to move his feet in a way she has never seen before.

At the end of the dance Miss MacColl came over to him.

'Where did you learn these setting steps?'

He was too frightened to answer, as if he were going to get a row.

'You're obviously a natural dancer,' she said.

When Marsaili asked Gille Ruadh about Bobby, he said, 'I'd be surprised if he wasn't a good dancer. His father had a sideboard full of cups.'

'What happened to him?' Marsaili asked, getting more and more intrigued with Bobby.

'He was killed in an accident. It's good to see that his talent lives on.'

After that Christmas party Bobby wasn't bullied. That was because he wasn't in the playground at the intervals. Miss MacColl took him in for dancing lessons, putting a dance band record on the player. She made the class stay out at the breaks, but they climbed up on the window sills to watch the woman with the big rump and the wee boy stepping round and round between the desks, holding hands to the music.

At the age of ten Bobby entered the dancing competitions in the Games. Marsaili sat on the hillside with her mother to watch him in the *Seann Triubhas*. It's a dance that's supposed to have been devised after the Forty Five Rebellion, when wearing the kilt was banned. The dancer shakes his legs as if getting rid of the despised trousers. Bobby was wearing a balmoral with a diced band, and his toes didn't seem to touch the platform as his arms moved above his head in a graceful sweep. It was Archie Maclean who announced through the loud-hailer that Bobby Lamont was the junior dancing champion. Marsaili and Alice met the victor going home with his mother on the back brae, the trophies clinking in the bag they carried between them. Alice hugged him, then straightened the big balmoral on his head.

'It was his father's balmoral,' Mrs Lamont explained. 'I kept it all those years because I just knew that the boy would be a good dancer too.'

Bobby left school at sixteen and became a joiner, 'a terrible waste,' the banker lamented as he filmed the apprentice going along the seafront with his canvas sling of tools to replace another rotting window sill in a holiday house. There was always a dance in the hall after the Games. It was a drunken affair, with young men lounging behind the building with half bottles of whisky before coming upstairs to throw their partners across the hall in an Eightsome Reel. But Bobby didn't drink, and every woman wanted to dance with him. As he was crossing the hall for a partner Marsaili's prayer was answered and he chose her. It was as if they were one body with four legs going round in the Highland Schottische, and when she looked over Bobby's shoulder she could see that the band were taking their timing from his feet.

When he walked her home that night Marsaili felt light-headed. She expected him to kiss her at the gate, but instead he shook her hand and asked, 'There's a dance on Friday. Would you like to go?'

They danced all over the island that summer, in little halls with their doors open on to the sea. They were never off the floor, from the first dance, when he held her arms behind her head in the Gay Gordons, until she closed her eyes and surrendered to his expert hold in the last waltz. He took her up to meet his thin nervous mother in their spartan cottage with its old-fashioned kitchen. There was a photograph of Bobby's father taken at the Games. Whoever was holding the camera must have moved because he came out blurred, in mid-air, with his diced stockings and trailing plaid, like a being dropping in from another world.

'You're seeing a lot of Bobby,' Archie MacLean said at the supper table.

'Do you think it's wise?' Alice asked.

'Why is it not wise?' Marsaili challenged her.

'Because you have to study.'

'It's the holidays, mother,' her daughter reminded her.

'Let her be,' the banker cautioned. 'Dancing never did anyone any harm. Besides, she's going to a house where she's hearing good Gaelic.'

'Is that all you care about, good Gaelic, Archie Maclean?' his wife said indignantly.

'It's become a rare commodity in this town and the Lamonts are decent people.'

'He's a joiner, Archie,' Alice reminded her husband.

'He's also a wonderful dancer, like his father. All he needs is a chance.'

One September evening they arranged to go to a dance at the other end of the island. Marsaili waited half an hour in the breezy evening for Bobby to come in a friend's car, and then she went upstairs.

'Never mind, dear,' her mother said consolingly. 'We'll have to start thinking about what you'll need for university. We'll go to the mainland to get clothes for you.'

A few nights later when her father came up to supper from his office he had news of Bobby.

'Evidently he was asked to go out to a yacht to repair a damaged rudder. I don't know the details, but they were dancing on the deck and he got involved. The owner's a television producer and apparently Bobby went with him to audition for a new show.'

In those days the television was black and white, and the picture was often turned into driving snow by bad weather at sea. But on the October night when the first programme in the new series about Scottish dancing was transmitted, the reception was as clear as it had ever been. There was Bobby, in kilt and pumps, dancing the Duke of Perth.

'He's made the big time now,' the banker said. 'His mother will be proud.'

That autumn Marsaili went to university in Glasgow to study veterinary science. It was a course that required a great deal of commitment, and she didn't go out much. One night Bobby Lamont appeared at her hall of residence.

'How can you show your face after standing me up?' she asked bitterly.

'I'm sorry, Marsaili, but everything happened so quickly. One minute I was repairing the rudder on the yacht, and the next I was sailing away on it. There's a dance at the Highlanders' Institute tomorrow night. Alasdair MacTavish is playing. Will you come so that I can make it up to you?'

Bobby looked into her eyes as he birled her in the Eightsome Reel. Marsaili knew that he wouldn't let her go and that no injury would happen to her. He drove her home in the new car he had acquired from the big money he was making as a dancer, and he kissed her before he opened the door of the hall of residence for her. Marsaili knew as she went up the staircase to her room with its spread of veterinary text books that she was in love.

They danced among other energetic exiles in the Highlanders' Institute every Friday night, and as he drove her home her head felt light. All night she dreamed that she was going round in his arms.

'I'm in love,' Bobby confessed as they were sitting waiting for the band to begin an evening of bliss.

Marsaili felt embarrassed. She was sure of her feelings for him, but she knew she would face the opposition of her mother, who was certain to remind her that she had a long haul in front of her before she qualified as a vet.

'Let's not talk about it now,' she asked him as she watched the accordionist strapping on his instrument.

'I *have* to talk about it to somebody,' he said. 'You'll understand. You've always understood, since that day at school when you helped me up from the floor of the porch and went to get Miss MacColl to attend to my leg.'

'I understand what you're saying, Bobby,' she said gently. 'But it's not possible.'

'I never thought *you* would say that, Marsaili.'

'But we have to be practical, Bobby. We both have careers.'

'But dancing's what brought us together,' he persisted. 'I'm in love.'

'And so am I, Bobby,' she told him, covering his hand. 'But it isn't the right time.'

'Why not?' He turned and signalled. A young man came across the floor.

'This is Michael.'

They shook hands. Marsaili was bewildered. What had Michael to do with Bobby being in love with her?

'Michael and I met on the set of the television show,' Bobby explained.

Marsaili remembered the fair-haired youth with steps more delicate than the woman he was dancing with. There had been many discussions at the supper table in the bank house, but never about men in love. In fact Marsaili couldn't remember an incident of it in the town, though there were plenty of adulterous affairs, as her father was always gleefully reminding his family. There had, however, been a female purser on the *Lochspelvie* who had rejected violently the advances of the local men and instead had sat in the Arms with her cropped hair, drinking pints and rolling her own smokes.

Bobby took Michael's hand. 'We're living together and we're very very happy. Promise me, Marsaili, that you'll keep it to yourself. It would kill my mother. She wants me to marry you. She said to me, if you get the banker's daughter you'll be a lucky man. You'll get everything you could desire – looks and brains. . . and Gaelic.'

Marsaili cried herself to sleep that night, but next evening Bobby was back at her door, asking her to go dancing. Michael was always there, so she had two partners to keep her feet moving until *Auld Lang Syne* was called. But her dreams were troubled. She would be doing a Pride of Erin waltz with Bobby when Michael would cut in, and it wasn't her he danced with.

'Are you coming home for Christmas?' she asked Bobby when they were sitting in a city café.

'I don't know what to do. I want to be with my mother, but I also want to be with Michael.'

'Take him,' she urged. 'Your mother will be pleased you have a friend, and in time she'll understand.'

'It's not her I'm worried about. It's what they'll say.'

'People won't bother, Bobby.'

'They'll bother all right. I suffered enough at school.'

'That's all in the past,' she told him.

He smiled wryly. 'I can see myself going along Main Street with Michael and them shouting poufs after us. It's a strange place, where we come from, Marsaili. They laugh at people having affairs, even though they're married, but when it comes to two men. . .'

'You *must* come home with Michael for Christmas,' she urged Bobby. 'They'll think you're just good friends.'

'Oh they'll know. They'll make it their business to know.'

'So I won't see you at the Christmas dance,' she said sadly.

A few nights later Marsaili was reading a book when she came across a quotation. It was from the Gnostic Gospels, and it said, 'To the Universe belongs the dancer. He who does not dance does not know what happens. Now if you follow my dance, see yourself in me.' She wrote the quotation in her Christmas card to Bobby.

The hall was decorated with balloons and tinsel, and Alasdair MacTavish and his band in their tartan jackets were on the stage. Marsaili hadn't heard from Bobby and assumed that he hadn't come home. She was asked up for the Gay Gordons, but the man held her arms roughly behind her head and trod on her toes. Then she saw Bobby and Michael coming in. They were wearing matching kilts. They kissed her and took their pumps from the holdall they were carrying between them. Alasdair MacTavish leaned towards the microphone and announced the Dashing White Sergeant.

Marsaili is in the middle, between Bobby and Michael. She is conscious that the ones who are sitting out, who were in school with them and who bullied Bobby, are watching enviously their setting steps and the way they weave in the reel of three. As they lift their arms and sweep on to join hands to make the next circle they are cheering. 'To the Universe belongs the dancer,' Bobby calls out as he turns Marsaili under his raised arm.

16.
The Officer's Mess

Major James (Jamie) Farquhar had ploughed thousands into the place, with little to show. He thought he would have inherited from his mother by now, but though she had had cobalt treatment for cancer, she was still holding on in the hotel in Harrogate, treating the staff like private servants.

The Major went to see Archie Maclean, to ask him to increase his overdraft. He told the banker that it would be perfectly safe because his nonagenarian mother had a huge shareholding in the armaments company that his father had set up.

The banker stood at the window, looking along Main Street. He had heard similar stories from other military men who had settled on the island.

'Perhaps you need to do something else with your place, Major,' he suggested.

'What do you mean?'

'Well, farming's never paid very well on this island. The ground's too poor, and the cost of taking animals to the sales too high.'

The Major went away and gave the matter serious consideration. One evening after dinner he saw the solution in a magazine. A mink farm. Next morning he phoned for a hundred. A few days later he took Annabel out to see them in the cages that Donald had built for them.

'What do you do with them?' Annabel asked.

'You feed them. Then they're killed for their fur. Couldn't be simpler,' the Major assured her.

The stevedores swore in Gaelic when the stinking bins came off the steamer from the fish buyer on the mainland. The Major reversed his tractor and trailer under the derrick and took delivery. He fed them himself, opening each cage and using a heavy leather glove to dole out the offal.

Captain Parkman had survived Changi on a diet of rice mixed in with rat shit. After a year in a sanatorium he arrived on the island because he had read about the therapeutic Hebrides. Farquhar used to go and drink a bottle of whisky with him. They never talked about the war. They talked about the Major's mink enterprise and the Captain's love of walking the mountains alone. He had recovered all the weight he had lost in captivity, and was feeling on top of the world. Before the war he had been at Bisley, but would never take up shooting again.

The Captain's hobby was bird watching. After a storm he would rise before dawn and walk out to the plantation, hoping for the sighting of a sheltering migrant. One morning he had seen a strange hawk sitting on a fence post. It was a red-footed falcon that should have been en route to Africa.

One night the Captain was out, looking for roding woodcock. He was crossing the bog to the whiffle of snipe when suddenly a light swept up the mountain, as if the sun had decided to rise again, having set so recently. Local poachers, using a head-lamp on a van roof to look for deer. The Captain began to tremble. He was back in the camp, the evening that the man had escaped, the searchlight sweeping the jungle, assisting the methodical Japs in the search. Parkman stumbled home through the bog, into the arms of his wife. That night his malaria returned, and he lost three stones in a month. Major Farquhar came to call, with a bottle of whisky.

'I've had enough,' Parkman sobbed.

'Give it time, Cecil,' the Major advised, pouring two bumpers of whisky. 'Another summer and you'll be fine.'

But his sleep was blinded by the arc-lamp, and the Jap soldier beat him with the rifle butt. One morning the bed was empty. His wife thought he had gone looking for birds, but his binoculars were hanging behind the door. They found his two-way hat at the edge of the bog.

Farquhar visited the Misses Huntingdales, two spinster sisters who had retired to the island. Molly had been a concert pianist, and had watched balefully as the baby grand was lowered in nets from the steamer. Her sister Astrid had been a surgeon in a London hospital, specialising in heart surgery. They bought an old house overlooking an estuary. Molly played Gaelic airs after dinner, while Astrid and the Major sat drinking whisky.

He was looking forward to realising a lot of money through selling the mink. He got up one morning to find the cages open. A thousand pounds had escaped. No, not escaped, they had been let loose. Farquhar began to suspect that it was Donald. He confronted him.

'And why the hell would I do a thing like that?' Donald asked furiously.

'Because you resent me as an incomer.'

'I never said anything like that.'

'I see it in your attitude.'

The couple went away. The Major had difficult replacing them, until some answered the newspaper advertisement.

Farquhar's next enterprise was growing daffodils. He was sure he could make a fortune, so a thousand bulbs came in sacks on the steamer, and he carried them down the gangway on his back himself. The spring show in the field around the house was spectacular. Annabel moved about in her bare feet, picking armfuls of daffodils which he took to the steamer, to send to the mainland market.

'We'll need to plant more for next season and send them further afield,' Farquhar told her as they were sitting drinking whisky on a summer evening. He had brought through the ledger to show that they had made a profit of four hundred pounds.

He planted the bulbs himself. On autumn evenings he drove to the hotel on his tractor, having a few drams with the locals and hearing about life in the past on the island, before he went home again, the tractor swerving across the road.

One morning he noticed black mounds in the fields of the daffodils. Moles had moved in. The mole catcher had to come from the north, and used poison. There were no daffodils the following spring, and Annabel was in despair.

'We don't seem to be having much luck on this island. Maybe it's time we moved back to the mainland.'

But he was determined to make a go of it.

'I'll do up the cottage over the winter and we can let it in the summer,' he proposed.

It was the original croft house. He laboured for the local mason who restored the fallen stones and put on a new roof. The Major himself varnished the pristine floors.

'It's beautiful,' Annabel enthused. 'I could live in it myself.'

They advertised in a magazine and received replies. It was soon booked up for July and August.

'It'll pay for itself in a couple of seasons,' the Major said.

His overdraft was now very high. Every week he went into the town to see Archie Maclean.

'And how is life with you?' the banker asked.

'I wish my mother would relinquish her hold on life, Archie.'

'What age is she?'

'Ninety three.'

'She must come from hardy stock.'

'She's got my father's money. When I get it I'll clear the overdraft and have a big credit balance.'

'Well, I shouldn't say this, but I hope that sad day – happy for my masters in Glasgow, of course – doesn't come too quickly,' the banker said, filling up his visitor's glass from the whisky bottle he kept in the bottom drawer of his filing cabinet.

'Sometimes I wonder,' the Major said, having had another snort.

The banker had had many types of people sitting in the chair occupied by the Major. He had had fishermen confessing their sins of fornication; he had had women reminiscing about torrid affairs they had had with visiting sailors during the war. On an island where there was ample time he never rushed his customers. Instead he turned towards the window and looked out over the bay, knowing that he was going to hear another confession.

'Sometimes I think I should have thought it out more,' the Major was saying, as if he were delivering a soliloquy. 'There was Helena, my first wife, standing at the drawing-room window, looking so lovely, and here was I, home to tell her that I was running off with another woman, one of her friends. I should have followed my feelings and fucked her and stayed.'

The banker was smiling wryly as he turned to his visitor.

'But Annabel's such a splendid woman.'

'Oh splendid,' the Major agreed. 'She's endured a lot since we came here – rats, those little bastards of mink escaping, and. . .'

But there was no need to complete the sentence. The banker had heard from others about the Major's infidelities, caught in the linen cupboard of the hotel with one of the maids. And there had been others, including the wife of Parkman, the Japanese camp victim. The Major had screwed his way round the island with the same charm that he employed at social gatherings.

'However, back to work,' he said, setting down his glass.

The Major got stout, and bandy-legged, and even more attractive to women. He continued to write out cheques for goods he couldn't afford on the expectation that his mother was about to breathe her last, but she hung on in Harrogate, bedridden, her memory, even of her son's name, gone. His children, now grown up, came to stay, one bringing a boyfriend who wore his hair to his shoulders.

He still went to the agricultural show, to judge the rams in the London Scottish kilt that was getting even more tattered, but walked out of the tent when the other drinkers had to be carried. He dreamed of going back to Cassino, but knew that the countess would be an old woman by now. Annabel's hair was grey. She had gone very quiet and was making baskets, sitting in her work-room at the window, staring out while her fingers worked the canes, an island Lady of Shallot.

The Major's overdraft was now 'astronomical', the term of abuse that the manager from Head Office used down the phone to Archie Maclean, who stood in his office, the instrument at his ear, looking out over the bay as he listened to the tirade. It was a dangerous thing to interrupt this man, who sat in an air-conditioned office high above a Glasgow street and knew nothing about island life.

'This overdraft must be reduced by a thousand by the end of the month. Do you understand, Maclean?'

'It will be, after he comes back from the Garden Party,' the banker assured him.

'What Garden Party?'

'The one Her Majesty gives at Holyrood Palace. Now I happen to know' – the banker dropped his voice – 'that our General Manager Mr Matheson would dearly love to be asked to the Garden Party. I've spoken about this possibility with Major Farquhar, and he's going to make a few discreet enquiries.'

stories from an island

A few miles along the coast was a Scottish Baronial castle embowered among trees above a bay. It belonged to a man who had had a large estate on the mainland, and who had been accused of interfering with a pageboy. To avert a scandal on royal Deeside his furniture was piled on a landing barge and he was told to go and make a new life for himself. Rounding Cape Wrath, the doleful hammers of the spinet that Mendelssohn had played on during his Scottish visit sounded, making the seals on the skerries raise their heads. The landing craft was run up on a sandy bay, the commode with the stained bowl that Queen Victoria has used, carried up to the house.

Sir James became very introverted. His wife went out horse riding. She and Major Farquhar met at a cocktail party and were irresistibly attracted to each other. The Major whispered the rendezvous, and next afternoon they met at the ruined township. Their horses drank from the burn as the Major pulled down her riding breeches. Twenty years of neglect were made up for that afternoon, and at dinner that night, her husband leaned across to pluck a frond of bracken from her hair. As she sat at the spinet, playing the Hebrides Overture for him, she was burning between the legs for the Major, and when her husband went upstairs early for his bath, she phoned him and arranged a meeting at the same place next afternoon.

The Major was in his sixties now. When he sat at a dance with his legs open, the women on the other side of the room stared before turning their faces away.

Rather than wait for his mother to die – she was almost due the royal telegram – the Major decided to sell his small estate. It was done on an impulse.

One afternoon an Australian presented himself at the door. He hoped he wasn't intruding, but he just *had* to see the place his ancestor had sailed from a hundred years before. The Major walked him up the hill to the ruins of the old crofting settlement, watching while the visitor put some of the soil into an envelope. Later, over whisky, he told the Major that the family had made good. He had a huge sheep farm. He wanted to come back. The deal was clinched.

The Major and Annabel built a Swedish log house on a piece of ground they had kept for themselves. When his mother died, instead of the legacy he needed to pay off his overdraft, there was debt.

17.
Broken Bones

A week before Halloween, Marsaili and her friend would go up the brae to Peter Maclean's croft to dig up turnips to make into lanterns. She still recalls those autumn nights under the stars, with a wind coming off the sea, tramping across the furrowed field with her prize under her arm. In the kitchen she sliced off the top and began to scoop out the contents.

You need patience as well as a sharp knife to make a good turnip lantern. Marsaili always cut out the eyes as triangles, and made two holes with the point of the knife for nostrils. That's when the face can give way. You don't have another turnip, and it's too far to go back up to the field.

On Halloween they dressed up in cardboard masks from the paper shop. Her friend Annie was always a witch, wearing a cone of black paper on her head, and carrying a broomstick, clumps of heather bound to a stick. They each had their lanterns under their arms, the faces glowing in the dark, as they went round the houses, doing their party pieces in return for fruits and money. Each year Marsaili would get an apple for singing a Gaelic song to old Mrs Maclean.

Then they went up the hill. Annie knocked on Muldonaich's door, and he would admit them to his sitting-room which seemed to be underground, because the top of the window was level with the street. One year he rattled a cardboard box on the mantelpiece.

'Do you know what's in there?' he asked.

The girls shook their heads.

'Bones.'

'That's not true,' Annie said, swallowing hard.

'It is true, and what's more, they're my bones.'

Marsaili started to giggle at the absurdity.

'I'm telling you the truth. It happened in South Georgia.'

They sat on his sofa to hear his story. He had been on the whalers. Marsaili winced as if the harpoon had struck her instead as he described how the whales were caught, then winched aboard the factory ship. Muldonaich described how the flensers had walked across the carcass, swinging their long-handled knives as if they were playing shinty on a hillock. He described all this factually, as if he had no feeling for the beauty and intelligence of these creatures of the ocean. They were only heaps of blubber to be harvested, their livers drained for the oil.

'So one day the carcass slipped and I was caught between it and the wall,' Muldonaich explained. 'They took me ashore and removed the broken bones from my body.'

'They mend bones, not remove them,' Annie pointed out.

'They removed mine,' he said, rattling the box and lifting the lid to show them.

'These aren't human bones,' Annie persisted.

Muldonaich came from a family that 'wasn't quite right', in Archie Maclean's oblique parlance, one of the many charms of his conversation. He never liked to speak ill of anyone, even though, as a bank manager, he had met some slippery characters, because, as he said, money brought out the worst in people.

Muldonaich had a brother who wandered about the town. He never attacked anyone, and was always polite, but he ended up in an institution on the mainland.

Muldonaich himself had gone to the whalers, and when he came back with his bones in the box he did odd jobs about the town. He never married, though Gille Ruadh remembered that he had had a relationship with one of the Johnstones, who had a deformed foot and liked a good dram.

So why did the two girls go guising to Muldonaich's house? Because it was mysterious. Apart from the box of his own bones, there was the tooth of a whale on a table, and other souvenirs he had brought back. Besides, he could do conjuring tricks which he had picked up from the Norwegian he had shared a berth with on the whaling ship.

Muldonaich's sitting-room was small, with a low ceiling, the floral paper grimy with the smoke that blew back down the chimney when the wind was from the north. A rickety old sofa's bare springs covered with a tartan travelling rug, full of holes. A very weak bulb in the lamp.

Muldonaich reaches behind his ear and produces an egg. He breaks its contents into a saucer and swallows it raw to the girls' disgust, then eats the shell. He puts his fingers into his mouth and produces the egg, whole.

Marsaili looks at the turnip lantern on the table beside her and sees the nostrils glowing. Beyond Annie's tall black hat is the box of the conjurer's bones on the mantelpiece, and for a moment Marsaili wonders if he can fit them back into his body.

Annie does a dance for the conjurer. She holds on to her tall hat as she weaves round and round the table, swaying her body as if casting a spell on the room. Muldonaich stands with his elbow on the mantelpiece, watching the performance as he smokes a cigarette, blowing the smoke out of his nostrils. Marsaili is thinking of the men walking across the murdered whale in their spiked boots, flailing its skin. Did it see Muldonaich out of the corner of its dying eye and raise a flipper to sweep him away, breaking his bones that ended up in a cardboard box?

The next Halloween Marsaili didn't go out with her friend because she had measles, and her mother wouldn't let her near the light. However, when she was no longer infective Annie came to see her. She had done the usual round at Halloween, including Muldonaich's.

'You went alone?' Marsaili queried.

'Yes. I wanted to see the bones again.'

'What trick did he do?'

Annie turned towards the high window overlooking the bay.

'Annie, what is it?' Marsaili called from her bed.

'He touched me.'

'Touched you?' she said, bewildered. Was it part of the trick?

'He touched me between the legs.'

'*Annie.*'

'He did,' she said vehemently, rounding on her friend.

'Did you tell your parents?'

Marsaili heard her parents talking in whispers. Muldonaich had been taken to the police station and charged with indecent assault. Dr Murdoch had examined Annie and pronounced that the hymen had been broken. Because he was a danger to the children of the town, Muldonaich was taken away on the steamer and remanded in custody to await trial. People shouted dire threats at him as he was pushed up the gangway in handcuffs.

Annie was kept off school, but Marsaili was allowed to go up to see her.

'My father says that Muldonaich will be sent to prison,' Marsaili told her to comfort her.

'That's too good for the bastard,' she said vehemently. 'He should be drowned.'

Annie was fifteen then, that same year that the first jukebox was winched off the cargo boat and conveyed along Main Street to the Sea Breezes Café. She was in the café night after night, feeding coins into the brightly lit console and watching mesmerised as the arm swung out the Buddy Holly single. Marsaili believes that she had one of the first miniskirts on the island, and she wore scarlet lipstick which Bessie in the chemist's had to send to the mainland for.

Annie smoked, and on nights when there was a dance at the hall she wasn't averse to taking a swig from one of the half bottles of whisky the youths had, to give them courage to get up on the floor. Marsaili had seen her falling in a Canadian barn dance, bringing her partner down as well, and she had assumed that Annie was the worse for drink.

Marsaili was seventeen when she went with her father to the asylum on the mainland where Muldonaich was confined. The banker needed to go there on business because one of his customers, Miss Mary MacKinnon, was a patient there. She had been peculiar for years, wearing two coats at the same time at the height of summer. Her house was so filthy that Dr Murdoch had certified her.

The banker was Miss MacKinnon's executor, and once again she wanted to change her will. One year she would leave all her money to cats, and then she would write her banker to say that she had gone off these animals, and would be making her bequest to a dogs' charity instead. The latest letter said that her money was going to endangered birds.

They took the car across on the ferry and drove down to the asylum. The banker was a long time inside, and Marsaili was asleep when he came out.

'I saw Muldonaich,' he said. 'It's pathetic. He's been getting electric shock treatment, and he was pleading with me to get him out of the place. I couldn't tell him that there was nothing I could do. I don't think he'll live much longer. And he's lost his Gaelic, because there's nobody there to speak it with.'

Meantime Annie was getting a reputation for 'being bad for men', another of Archie Maclean's polite phrases. She broke up the Macfarlanes' marriage, having been discovered in bed with Jimmy by his wife. She was drinking so heavily that her liver was damaged.

'To think that she's come to this after what Muldonaich did to her,' Alice told her daughter. 'She was such a lovely girl. Do you remember when she came up here at Halloween in her witch's costume?'

How could Marsaili forget the conical black hat, the grinning mouth of the turnip lantern? How could she forget Muldonaich's bones rattling in the box?

Annie drowned in the bay. Some said that she was drunk and stumbled in her high heels as she looked for a fisherman to have sex with. Others said that it was suicide, because she couldn't live with the memory of what had been done to her as a girl guiser.

A week after the funeral Annie's mother came into the bank to see Archie Maclean, and an hour later he came upstairs to the house. He handed his wife a letter, and as she read it she put her hand over her mouth.

'Her mother's asking me what she should do.'

The letter was handed to Marsaili, because she was now old enough to understand these things.

> I wish it to be known that Muldonaich did not touch
> me that night when I went up to his house alone.
> I made up the story because he wouldn't give me any
> money for cigarettes.   (Signed) Annie MacKay

'So what do I do ?' the banker asked his wife and daughter. 'Do I tell that poor soul downstairs to tear up the letter and forget about it?'

'I don't think you can do that,' Marsaili cautioned him. 'Annie left this letter so that it would be found. She wanted the truth to come out. Muldonaich's been in the asylum all these years for something he didn't do. This letter's bound to get him released.'

'Think of the trouble it will cause in the town,' Alice came in. 'What kind of memory will they have of Annie? After all, Muldonaich's an old man.'

Mrs MacKay went up the brae to the police station and handed over the letter. The banker had shut up Muldonaich's house when he was taken into custody. Marsaili and he went up the hill one evening and unlocked it. The place reeked of damp and the wallpaper was coming away like a soiled bandage. They opened the windows and mopped the floors. Marsaili lifted the lid of the box of bones on the mantelpiece where Muldonaich had stood, talking about the brutal flensers walking the back of the butchered whale.

'He should be home any day,' her father said as he got a fire started in the grate, but the wind was from the wrong direction that day and filled the low room with smoke. The banker took a half bottle of whisky from his pocket and stood it beside the box of bones, as a coming home present.

Marsaili went down to the steamer every day but Muldonaich didn't come off it. The banker phoned Dr Murdoch to ask his advice, because he didn't know what to do about the house.

'He's coming home next week,' Archie informed his family when he came up from his office.

There was a bigger crowd than usual on the steamer, which was late because of the heavy swell out in the sound. Muldonaich looked much older and thinner, as if he had lost even more bones.

He was accompanied by a nurse from the asylum who was carrying the case he had gone away with all those years before, when the first jukebox had arrived on the island. People drew back as he set foot on the pier, as if they were ashamed. Only the banker went forward to shake his hand, to welcome him back to the island.

Muldonaich had a home help, who came in every day to make his meals and to set the temperamental fire. He was fit enough, but didn't venture out. Marsaili and her father went up to see him. Archie tried speaking with him in Gaelic, but it seemed that the electric shock treatment had driven his native language out of his skull. Nor did he speak about his whaling days.

They were Muldonaich's only visitors. Why was this? Marsaili asked her father. He thought it was because the older people who had known him well had died while he was away in the asylum. But he also thought there was something else.

'They still feel he was guilty.'

Muldonaich's death was a deliverance. The banker and his daughter cleared the house, which was being sold, and the money given to the Lifeboats. Marsaili took down the box of bones and rowed out of the bay on a calm evening, dumping them into the deep.

18.
The Speywife

On Saturday afternoons Marsaili helped out in the Sea Breezes Café for pocket money. An old stooped woman in a frayed coat from down the island always came into the café for a cup of tea and a roll and butter. Marsaili was frightened by the way her rheumy eyes watched her from under the brim of her old-fashioned hat, but Mrs Bonelli served her and sat talking to her at a corner table. She wouldn't take the money from the old woman and helped her on to the bus with her bags.

Cairistiona and Marsaili went to university together and were next door to each other in the hall of residence in Glasgow. Marsaili wanted to go dancing at the Highlanders' Institute at the weekends, especially when Alasdair MacTavish was playing, but Cairistiona was very studious. Though her closest friend never said so, Marsaili knew that Cairistiona felt she had an obligation to her father to succeed, since she was the only child.

Marsaili worked in the Sea Breezes Café in the summer while Cairistiona studied upstairs.

'I think we should go for a walk tonight,' Marsaili would call up, and back would come the reply, 'Too busy!'

'She's too pale,' Mrs Bonelli said.

'Let her be,' Joe beamed. 'She wants to be a good doctor. Marsaili, take her up this ice cream.' He always put a cherry on top.

One autumn evening in their second year Cairistiona knocked on Marsaili's door in the hall of residence.

'Don't tell me the greatest swot on earth is taking a break,' Marsaili said light-heartedly.

Cairistiona was lifting her sweater above her head and unhooking her bra. Was this why Cairistiona Stella Bonelli didn't have a boyfriend? Marsaili's friend stood in front of her with her beautiful breasts, her hair hanging down her back.

She took Marsaili's hand and placed it on her breast. Marsaili tried to pull it away.

'I'm very fond of you, but not in that way,' she told her. 'Please put your clothes back on.'

'I don't mean that,' she said. 'Here.' She moved Marsaili's hand. 'Is there a lump?'

'How long have you had it?' Marsaili asked as she felt its hard smallness.

'I only noticed it tonight, when I was having a shower.'

'Then it's nothing to worry about,' Marsaili assured her.

'I'll go and see about it in the morning,' she said.

Marsaili made them coffee and they sat cross-legged on the floor, reminiscing about their upbringing on the island. Cairistiona kissed her friend goodnight before she closed the door.

She was back in Marsaili's room the next night.

'The doctor doesn't think the lump's malignant. He's referred me to the infirmary for tests.'

'That's good news,' Marsaili said. 'Now why don't we go out to the cinema?'

Cairistiona disappeared out of Marsaili's life for about a fortnight because of her exams, and when she passed her room late she would see the golden line of her reading lamp under the door. Then one night when she was getting ready to go out to a party, there was a knock on her door.

'The surgeon's suspicious of the lump,' Cairistiona said. 'I have to go to hospital to have a biopsy. Will you come with me?'

They walked hand in hand along the street, as they had done when they were in primary school at home. Marsaili waited for two hours while one woman after another came out. But still Cairistiona wan't coming. A nurse appeared and said that Cairistiona wanted to see her. She was sitting in a side-room, holding a small pad against her breast.

'They took a needle biopsy.'

'What's that?' Marsaili asked, scared.

'They take out a core of the lump to test it.'

'When will you get the result?'

'I have. It's malignant. You know, it's a strange thing. I've sectioned the breasts of women with tumours in the anatomy room, yet I feel squeamish about my own.'

Cairistiona's exams coincided with her radiotherapy treatment, and she had to ask the Professor for a postponement. One night she came into Marsaili's room to show her the little blue cross that the radiotherapist had made on her breast, near her heart, where the ray was to be directed.

'It looks like a stigmata, the kind that saints get,' Cairistiona said.

'You're very brave,' Marsaili said, hugging her.

'Not brave – scared.'

Every morning for six weeks Marsaili insisted on accompanying her friend to the hospital. The radiation treatment only lasted a few minutes, but there were a lot of women in the queue, and sometimes Marsaili waited for half an hour.

'I hate that place,' Cairistiona said when she emerged. 'It's so bare, so souless. Why don't they put a few paintings on the walls, and a few flowers in vases?' She confronted her friend on the street. 'You're going home for the holidays next week.'

'I'll stay with you,' Marsaili told her.

'No, you must go. Tell my parents that I'm getting experience, working in a hospital.'

On her first night back Marsaili went to the Sea Breezes Café where the new jukebox was playing numbers she didn't recognise. As she had a coffee with the Bonellis she told them how well their daughter was doing, and how sorry she was that she couldn't get home this holiday, but the chance had come up in the hospital to work with her Professor, and it was too good to turn down.

'She's a wonderful girl,' Joe said, shaking his head, still in awe that he had managed to produce such a daughter, after the vicissitudes of wartime internment.

'Thank God she's got you as a friend in Glasgow,' Mrs Bonelli said. 'You're like another daughter to us, Marsaili.'

Cairistiona came home for the summer vacation and worked the espresso machine, an apron round her hips. She was dressing one night when her mother came into her room.

'What's that?' she asked, pointing to the blue mark on her daughter's breast.

Cairistiona had to think very quickly.

'It's a tattoo I had done.'

'That's a pity, because it spoils your beautiful breasts.'

'It's a religious sign,' her daughter pointed out.

A week before Christmas Cairistiona came into her friend's room and told her that the previous day she had gone to the hospital for a check-up, and that they had discovered another lump in the same breast.

'They're going to remove the breast,' she revealed, clinging to

stories from an island   147

Marsaili. 'My parents are expecting me home. Will you go and see them and make an excuse? I know it's a big thing to ask you, but I can't face telling them because it'll destroy them.'

Joe was frothing milk at the machine when Marsaili came in from the windy autumn night.

'So where is she?' he asked eagerly.

'She's not coming,' Marsaili said.

Joe looked bewildered and called up the stairs for his wife. 'She has a boy friend? Joe said.

'A young doctor,' Marsaili hinted, and Joe beamed as Val Dooni-can crooned from the lighted jukebox at their backs.

'I don't believe that,' his wife said. 'Tell me the truth, Marsaili.'

She told them that their daughter had cancer. Val Doonican fell silent and Joe started to weep.

'I didn't struggle through the war on my own to give up now,' his wife rebuked him. 'Marsaili, I'm coming along the street with you to ask your father a big favour.'

She wanted to be driven thirty miles down the island to the Ross the next afternoon. The banker took her, and Marsaili sat in the back. They seemed to be on a deserted road for miles till they came to a small house with a corrugated iron roof. Mrs Bonelli went inside.

'What is this place called?' Marsaili asked her father.

'*Camas nan Geall*, the bay of the stranger,' Archie said. 'Gille Ruadh was talking about it one night in the house. There are the ruins of a beehive cell on the shore. A holy man's supposed to have lived there, but nobody knows his name. These anchorites were all over the Hebrides, Marsaili. They lived on flounders and faith.'

Ten minutes later Marsaili saw the same old stooped woman who came into the café on Saturdays, coming shuffling out of the house and going up on to the moor.

'Who is she?' she asked her father.

'We'll ask Gille Ruadh when he comes up tonight.'

'That's Jeannie Beaton. She's a speywife,' their visitor informed them as he slid open the Gold Flake pack, offering the first to his hostess, with a light to follow.

'What's a speywife?' Marsaili asked.

'Someone with special powers,' Gille Ruadh explained. 'Jeannie Beaton is not a woman to get on the wrong side of. One of her neighbours on the Ross had the evil eye put on his cattle because he swore at her.'

'John, I'm going to tell you something because I trust you,' the banker began. 'We took Mrs Bonelli down to see Jeannie this afternoon. Cairistiona the daughter has breast cancer. Jeannie took her up on the moor behind the house, and when Mrs Bonelli came back to the car she had plants with her. What was it she said to you, Marsaili?'

'I'm coming to Glasgow with you tomorrow.'

'Will Joe manage the café himself?' the banker had asked Mrs Bonelli as he drove her home.

'I managed it myself in the war. It's his turn now.'

When Marsaili phoned her father to tell him what had happened he wouldn't believe it. Mrs Bonelli had gone into the ward where Cairistiona was and demanded to see the specialist.

'You are not removing my beautiful daughter's breast,' she told him.

'She has a malignant tumour, Mrs Bonelli. The breast has to come off. There's no alternative.'

'Yes there is,' she told him, rummaging in her bag and producing a fistful of plants.

She stayed in Cairistiona's room in the hall of residence, though it was against the rules, and she used the communal kitchen to boil the plants she had got from the speywife, draining the green juice from them into a bottle. Marsaili went to the hospital with her and she made the nurse sit Cairistiona up. When she tried to spit it out her mother spoke sharply to her. 'There's no alternative.'

Every Friday a badly tied brown paper parcel arrived at the hall of residence, addressed to Mrs Bonelli in a child's handwriting, and that night she boiled up the plants and took the juice to the infirmary. She was Marsaili's neighbour in the hall of residence.

Twenty years on, Marsaili and Douglas had Cairistiona and her husband Tom to dinner in their Glasgow home. Theirs is a medical marriage. Cairistiona is a consultant gynaecologist and he is an anaesthetist. Sometimes they work together, assisting difficult births. Their daughter, also named Cairistiona, is at Edinburgh University with Marsaili's daughter.

The conversation at table was about the old days in the Sea Breezes Café.

'Your father was so good to my parents,' Cairistiona said.

'They were good people,' Marsaili told her. 'It was a happy place. What a pity the new English owners changed it. There's no jukebox now, and not the same characters like old Mrs Beaton from down the island who came in on a Saturday.'

Marsaili said this without thinking. Cairistiona looked up from her plate. 'Mother made me drink that awful stuff, day in, day out. Then they took me to X-ray and the tumour had gone. They were sure the machine was faulty, so I was taken to the machine at the Royal. The results were the same, no trace of the cancer. I was trained as a doctor to have faith in science. I don't know if I want to believe that that awful stuff from the speywife got rid of my cancer, but I don't have any other explanation.'

Marsaili put the casserole on the table and lifted the lid.

'What's this?' Cairistiona asked.

'Chanterelles.'

'Where on earth did you get them?'

Marsaili looked at the yellow medallions floating in gravy.

'I picked them myself when I was home last weekend. Don't you remember, your mother showed us where they grew?'

Marsaili could have told her friend something else from the past. When the banker told Gille Ruadh in the greatest confidence about the herbal cure, he wasn't surprised. 'They're the same family who were physicians to the Lords of the Isles,' he said before he offered his hostess a Golf Flake and a flame.

19.
Sunset Court

Dolina Macdonald was one of these people who conduct their business in public. When she bought the old fishing tackle shop on Main Street she told the world how much she was having to borrow to convert it into the Spinnaker Restaurant.

'That coffee machine cost a thousand pounds,' she informed her first customers. 'I'm paying eight per cent interest on it to the bank. And these tables cost over two thousand. All in all I've spent eight thousand converting this place and I'm up to *here* in debt.' She held a level hand at her throat.

Some of the locals wondered if they were being told this so that they would give her their custom instead of going to the Creel, the other restaurant on Main Street which baked its own scones and where the woman who owned it, and who was separated from her husband, hardly spoke a word as she poured out her bitter brew. This suited people who wanted to go in to read a newspaper or converse with friends.

But Dolina was a local, born and bred, and they felt that they had to support her, to buy cups of frothy coffee and little cakes from boxes of six that came off a van. Every sip and bite they took was helping to reduce her debt, or so they believed.

When the bank rate went up Dolina announced to half a dozen customers on a rainy morning that she might have to close. This embarrassed Marsaili Maclean, who had a summer job in the Spinnaker. Her father the banker had advanced Dolina the money, so Marsaili was the one who had to listen to Dolina the most. She insisted that Marsaili wear a white apron down to her shins, like a garçon in a Parisian café, though Dolina had never been to that city and couldn't speak a word of French. Gaelic was Dolina's native language, and she went about muttering to herself about the woes of the world as she put more Mr Kipling cakes into the glass counter, or raised the dripping basket of chips from the bubbling oil, tipping them on to the ashet where the deep fried haddock, deep frozen, lay under a wedge of lemon, beside a sad little curl of lettuce and one transparent slice of cucumber. Marsaili was ashamed to put it in front of the hiker, but he took five minutes to finish it and left her fifty pence under the rim of his plate.

Marsaili wasn't allowed to keep these tips. There was a jar she shared with Dolina, and she would have felt guilty about putting the coin under her long apron because she was beginning to feel partly responsible for her employer's huge debt, and each time a coin clinked into the jar Marsaili had the satisfaction of thinking that it was going to that purpose.

When the place was quiet Dolina and her assistant sat drinking coffee.

'If the bank rate goes up again I'm finished,' was her daily theme, though Marsaili knew by the number of customers that she was doing all right.

One afternoon an elderly man came in and sat down by the window. He was wearing a pearl-grey stetson which he laid on the table before he took spectacles out of a steel case and examined the menu in its brown cover. Marsaili went across with her pad and pen to hear what he would like.

'Is the fish fresh?' he asked.

Marsaili was taken aback, not by the substance of the question, but because it was delivered in Gaelic. She looked across, but Dolina was in the kitchen.

'The fish isn't fresh,' Marsaili responded in Gaelic. 'It's difficult to get fresh fish every day.'

'It wasn't in my time,' the customer said. 'I've seen so many boats in the harbour, you could walk across the decks.'

'When was that?' Marsaili enquired, genuinely interested. It was the kind of Gaelic conversation her father loved to have.

'Long before you were born, lassie,' he said. 'Frozen fish. It could be from anywhere in the world.'

'I suppose so,' Marsaili said.

'What is lasagne?' he asked, studying the menu again.

'*That's* home-made,' the waitress said with relief.

'Yes, but what is it?'

'It's mince with cheese on top.'

He made a face. 'I've never eaten both off the same plate. When I was young here, cheese went with bread and mince with potatoes. It's like Gaelic; it's getting filled up with foreign words.'

'Would you like to try the lasagne?' Marsaili suggested.

He shook his head. 'Bring me a cup of tea and a roll with butter.'

Marsaili buttered the roll herself, thinking that it wasn't going to help much towards Dolina's interest payments. She came through from the kitchen, glancing at the man who was sitting looking out of the window.

'He wanted fresh fish,' Marsaili whispered to Dolina.

She became irate when her menu was criticised.

'I hope you told him we can't get fresh fish till the boats come in on Friday.'

'I told him, but he said there was plenty when he was a boy here.'

Dolina called across the counter.

'Excuse me, but is something not to your liking?'

When the man turned she dropped the plate.

'My God,' she said. 'Uncle Alasdair.'

He hugged her and held her at arm's length.

'The last time I saw you, you were going to be a nurse.'

'I was young then,' she said, sitting down beside him. 'I lost the notion.'

'When did you open this place?' he asked.

'About a year ago. Have you just arrived?'

'I came last night. I'm staying up at the Hebridean.'

'You should have let me know you were coming,' Dolina told him. 'I've got a spare room.'

'I wanted to come back quietly, to see how things were. At least you picked a helper who can speak Gaelic.'

'That's the banker's daughter.'

'I must go and see him about transferring funds,' Uncle Alasdair said. 'How are you getting on?'

'I had to borrow a lot to start this place, and I don't know if I'm going to make it,' his niece told him. 'I'm due over ten thousand to the bank.'

Marsaili wondered why the debt had suddenly increased.

'It's a big commitment,' he conceded.

'Are you going back out to Canada?' Dolina asked her uncle.

He shrugged. 'I don't know. I could have retired ten years ago, but I kept working in real estate. It wasn't the money, but to give me something to do in life.'

It was four o' clock when Marsaili finished. She folded her apron on the counter and said cheerio in Gaelic to both of them.

'Dolina's uncle from Canada appeared today,' she told her parents over supper. The banker ceased cracking the crab claw in his fingers.

'So the Bootlegger's back. She'll be all right now.'

'Why do you call him the Bootlegger?' Marsaili asked.

'I've heard about him. Gille Ruadh will tell us all about him tonight.'

A Gold Flake was pulled from the packet, the stick supporting an ankle.

'Alasdair used to work on the pier, helping to unload the cargo boats. Then one day he disappeared. The pier master thought he'd fallen in and was going to call the navy to send a diver, but one of the other stevedores had seen him going up the gangway of a yacht that had crossed the Atlantic. Apparently he'd been taken on as a crew member for the return journey, or maybe they were giving him a lift. This is the nineteen twenties I'm talking about. They say that Alasdair went to Chicago and got in with the bootleggers.'

'As a Gael of few words he was presumably valuable for delivering lorryloads of hooch,' the banker suggested.

When prohibition was lifted the Bootlegger moved into Canada. Some said that he went into the fur trade, because he appeared back on the island just after the war in a magnificent coat with a beaver collar and a book of American Express travellers' cheques.

'He told the Gille Ruadh himself about his interests in real estate.'

'What's real estate?' Marsaili queried.

'Land and buildings,' her father explained. 'The kind of investment that bankers love. Dolina will be all right because she's his last living relative. She may end up owning a skyscraper as well as the Spinnaker.'

The Bootlegger was in the café every day, having his lunch. Dolina told Marsaili not to take the money from Uncle Alasdair. But what about the interest? Marsaili wanted to ask. The Bootlegger even acquired a liking for lasagne. His pearl-grey hat lay beside the pepper and salt as he ate, and he would finish with his niece's apple pie, with its spiced segments and golden crust. The place was busy with summer visitors who never asked if the haddock was fresh, and who forked up the lasagne even on hot days when salad was available.

Marsaili noticed that when the Bootlegger was in, his niece no longer broadcast her interest burden.

'Uncle's not going back to Canada,' Dolina told her one quiet morning. 'He's moved in with me. It's just as well, rather than paying these prices in the Hebridean.'

Marsaili relayed this news to her father, who was taking a particular interest in the Bootlegger.

'That's him caught now,' he predicted. 'It's only a matter of time before the café's paid off and she has a new car to drive both of them up and down the brae.'

But there wasn't any new car, and the Bootlegger continued to eat his lunch at the window table, where the Reserved sign was put on between twelve and two, though there were three other chairs at that table.

'I met the Bootlegger today,' the banker reported at supper. 'We had a long conversation in Gaelic. I find it gratifying that he's held on to his native language like that. You would hardly think he'd been away from the place, except for the slight Canadian burr. He was telling me that he has a piece of real estate in Montreal they want to build a supermarket on, but he's not selling until the bid goes up. And to think that he began here pushing sacks of flour on a barrow.'

Marsaili was lifting away his plate when the Bootlegger spoke to her in Gaelic.

'What are you going to do when you leave university?'

'A vet. I'm hoping to come back here to practise.'

'Don't,' he warned, fingering the indented crown of his wide hat. 'Go to Canada, the land of opportunity. There are huge herds of cattle out there and thousands of horses. You'll make a fortune as a vet.'

'But will there be Gaelic?' she asked.

'Even if you don't find someone to talk it to you never lose your Gaelic. Look at me, fifty years away, and I've got more words than my niece.'

Almost every day now he asked for the lasagne, followed by the apple pie, and he would drink two cups of strong black coffee. Dolina was in a temper, slapping about utensils in the kitchen when Marsaili came in one morning.

'I could kill the Chancellor of the Exchequer,' she raged. 'He's gone and put the interest rate up by one per cent because he feels the economy's overheating. Well my phone will be overheating when your father comes on from the bank to ask me what I'm going to do about my overdraft. Oh I know it's not his fault. He's got Head Office breathing down his neck.'

Archie Maclean liked his daughter to relay the conversations of the day in the café over supper, as if she were a spy for his bank.

'I bet the Bootlegger's signing the cheque for Dolina's loan – *and* the extra interest – right now,' he said.

But the next day the Spinnaker's best customer didn't come to the window table, though it was reserved for him.

'Is your uncle ill?' Marsaili asked Dolina.

She was working at the hissing coffee machine.

'If he shows his face in here again, charge him the full price.'

Marsaili didn't like to ask her what had happened, but her father had the answer that evening over their mackerel in oatmeal. It was not a dish that his children enjoyed, but he urged them to eat it, not so much for the nutrition, but to remind them that the plentiful fish was part of the staple diet of the island, in the days when people were poor.

'The Bootlegger is in Sunset Court,' the banker announced as he shook salt over his fish, trawled that afternoon off the lighthouse by one of his customers.

Sunset Court was the old folks' home at the top of the town.

'But that will cost him a fortune. Dolina will be furious,' Alice, who was not given to gossip, said.

'Not at all. The state is paying for him because his niece put him out.'

'But why would she do that?' Marsaili asked, shocked.

'Because when it came to writing the cheque for the interest, he didn't have the wherewithal. There is no real estate in Montreal, and I suspect that the collar of that coat, far from being beaver, was fake. The Bootlegger has no money.'

'But he *must* have paid his bill at the Hebridean, when he came here at first,' Marsaili pointed out.

'A clever trick to get his niece to take him in and feed him, then evict him so that he has to get a place in Sunset Court. '

'But *you* were also taken in,' Marsaili pointed out. '*You* thought he was wealthy.'

'Yes I did, which shows what a clever man he is.'

The bank rate has gone up again, and Dolina is sitting at the window in her uncle's chair, telling her regular customers that she's close to ruin, though Marsaili knows the season she's had by the fullness of the tips jar. Marsaili goes back to university next week and will not consider a career in Canada.

As for the Gille Ruadh, he isn't surprised by the Bootlegger's manipulation of his niece.

'They always were a tricky family,' he pronounces as he presents his hostess with her weekly Black Magic.

20.
Peaches

Flora was watched every minute of the day by her two brothers in case she absconded again. They wouldn't leave her alone at the house while they were out fishing, so they took her with them in the launch. She was expected to help with hauling in the net, and when they got back home, while they boxed the salmon for dispatch on the boat, she prepared the supper.

When they went to town for provisions she walked between them and was never let out of their sight. One of them went into the chemist's with her when she bought her supply of sanitary towels. They were even watchful of her when they went to the bank. Archie Maclean had heard how she had run away to the mainland, and been snatched from the hotel where she was working as a waitress. In the story that had reached him, they had bound her hands and feet with a length of rope from the boat, before carrying her aboard, shouting and swearing at them.

They stood behind her chair while they did their business. Her eyes conveyed to the banker that she was biding her time, and wouldn't need any help from the outside world. When he went upstairs to his family, he told them that he expected to hear of murder done at that lonely primitive house.

They made her sleep between them and took turns in having sex with her. There was no tenderness, and she didn't resist because then they would have used force. She thought of Aldo, holding her so carefully on the dance floor. She thought of the heat and brightness of Sicily, to where he was returning at the end of the season.

She hardly spoke to her brothers, though they tried to make conversation. Every night in her bed, before either of them took her, she clenched her fists and prayed that something would happen to the two of them. She prayed so hard that her nails bloodied her palms.

A year after she had been brought back home Iain was eating his supper one evening when he suddenly stood up, the cutlery still in his fists. He was staring at the door as if a ghost had just come in.

'What's wrong?' his twin asked.

He pitched forward across the table, his face cut by a broken plate. When they laid him on the floor and opened his shirt there was no heart beat. She turned towards the stove with a smile while the other brother was weeping over the corpse.

The banker was at his window when he saw the launch coming in with only the two of them. He ran up the stairs, and his wife and Marsaili crowded into the turret window as they watched the woman and her brother carrying the body up the slipway to the undertaker's store. It wasn't a suitable occasion for the cine camera.

The coffin came off that evening's boat, and they took it back with them in the launch to their habitation, carrying it like a fishbox into the house, where it lay between two chairs. Flora went about her work, cooking and cleaning, as if it weren't in the room.

But when she set down a cup of tea for her surviving brother on the coffin he swept it to the floor where it smashed round her feet.

'Have some respect,' he told her savagely.

'How can I have respect for him, the way he treated me?' she answered with equal anger. 'I'm glad the bastard's in there.'

The next blow sent her across the room, and she almost staggered into the fire.

'Don't think you'll get away,' he told her.

'Oh I'll get away. One way or another, I'll get away.' Her Gaelic was magnificent in her vehemence.

Murchison the Minister told the banker about the bleakest funeral he had ever been asked to officiate at – only the brother and sister at the grave in the remote chapel which, legend claimed, had never been able to keep its roof, not because of its proximity to the sea, but because of the Devil's doing.

When he went out fishing he took her with him, and would never turn his back on her in case she pushed him into the sea. He knew by the hatred in her expression that she was capable of anything.

She was his slave. He continued to use her in bed, and sat at the table, waiting for the plate to be put in front of him. When they went round the headland to the town for provisions he wouldn't let her out of his sight for a second.

He was getting slower. The biting chill of the ocean had got into a hip. He walked with pain, but wouldn't consider going round to see Dr Murdoch. It got so bad that he could no longer get on top of her. When he tied up the launch at its moorings for the night he took a vital part out of the engine, because he knew that he wouldn't be able to catch her if she ran out.

The arthritis was in his hands now, and they began to look like the barnacles he and his brother used to scrape from the launch when they beached it every few years, to paint the bottom with anti-fouling. During the night he cried out in pain.

He couldn't hold the hammer and nails to box the salmon, and had to stand over her while she did it. He couldn't manage to shave, but knew that he daren't put his cut-throat razor in her hands, so he grew a grey beard, which made him look even more stern and biblical.

'I'm sorry for the way things have been,' he said to her suddenly after supper, having tried unsuccessfully to light his pipe.

'You're sorry because of the state you're in,' she said without pity. 'Look at you; your sides are caving in like the old boat along the shore. It's your punishment for the way you've treated me.' She got up and looked into the mirror, its silvering streaked by the dampness. 'I could have made something of myself. I could have lived with a decent man and had children, not with two bastards who used me like a prostitute.'

'I said I was sorry,' he repeated at her back.

Over her shoulder she could see him in the mirror. 'It'll get worse,' she warned him. 'It'll get a lot worse, because I put a curse on you.'

'You did *what?*'

'I put a curse on both of you, when I was in bed between the two of you, and you had both used me. I had the seed of my own brothers inside me and I said to myself, you don't do this to dogs. Since God hasn't answered my prayers, I'll just have to try Satan himself, I said. I asked him to take away the first of my tormentors, and that's what happened. Then I asked for the second one to be taken, but this time I asked for it to be a slow, painful end.'

'You're a wicked woman,' he shouted, rising from his chair.

She hurried across to the cupboard where he kept the gun for shooting the seals that interfered with the nets, and turned the barrels on him.

'I could shoot you here and now and put you out of your misery.'

'You wouldn't get away with it.'

'Oh yes I would. I would take the boat round to town and tell the banker that you had fallen overboard and that the body had been washed out to sea. I know the way he looks at me, he knows the hellish life I've had with the two of you. Even if he didn't believe my story he would support me.

'But I'm not going to put you out of your misery, and I'm not going to run away, which I could easily do, because these legs wouldn't bring me back a second time. I'm staying here. I'll help you to land the salmon and I'll cook for you, and if you want my body you can have it, because it's meaningless to me, like gutting a fish. But you're going to have to put the account in my name as well.'

As he got more crippled it was she who was at the helm of the launch when it swept into the bay past Archie Maclean's window. It was she who did the shopping and paid the cheques in at the bank.

'Here's your supper,' she said one night, and put the plate on the floor for him.

'You're a callous woman.'

'Come and get it,' she told him, pushing the plate with her foot as if he were a dog.

He came across the flagstones on his ruined knees and crouched, tearing the fish with his hands because he could no longer hold a knife and fork.

'And your tea,' she said, pouring it into a bowl beside the plate.

He cried out in pain during the night, and one morning he couldn't get out of bed.

'I'm not taking the nets out,' she told him. 'You're going to have to go into the Home in the town.'

'Please keep me here,' he pleaded. 'I want to die in my own bed. Please. I'm sorry the way I treated you, and I'll make it up to you.'

'You make it up to me? Look at the state of you. If we had a dog like that we would put it out of its misery.'

'Then put me out of my misery,' he pleaded, pointing to the cupboard where they kept the gun.

'You're not getting out of it so easily, like that other bastard. You're going into the Home in the town.'

'Please keep me here, Flora. I want to die here, in my own bed.'

'You'll die in the Home, knowing nobody,' she told him. 'You'll never hear Gaelic again nor see the sea again.'

When the launch swept into the bay he was lying in the bottom. She phoned the doctor from the kiosk, and the ambulance came and took him up to Sunset Court. Archie Maclean had run up the stairs for his cine camera. He missed the ambulance taking her brother away, but caught her coming out of the shop with a big tin of peaches and a tin opener. She stood at the railing, eating the rosy yellow fruit with her fingers, then drinking the rich syrup as the banker filmed her from his tower.

Before first light next morning the passing trawler saw the fire at the house on the headland. An hour later the launch came into the harbour. She was holding down her dress in the blowy day as she went along to the bank.

'What happened?' the banker asked as he took her into his office.

'The house went on fire.'

'I don't think your brothers insured it,' Archie warned her.

'It wasn't worth insuring. It was a hovel.'

'We'll need to get you a house in the town, to be near your brother,' he suggested.

'No, I'm going away. I came to draw some money. That's in order, isn't it?'

'Oh yes, the account's in your name as well as your brother's.'

'How much is in it?'

'Forty thousand.'

'I'll take a thousand – in cash.'

'You could be robbed,' he said, worried.

She stared at him.

He had to go upstairs to the house for a carrier bag for the money. She went on the nine o' clock bus with the old suitcase she had salvaged from home. The banker knew that she was somewhere in Glasgow, because that was where she was drawing money from the account. Within a year there was very little left in it. When her brother died in Sunset Court they tried to contact her, but the letter came back: 'Gone Abroad.'

21.
The Other World

Dr Kenneth Murdoch was a Licentiate in Medicine, a phrase that Marsaili found erotic. Her father explained that it was a certificate of competence, rather than a medical degree. Dr Murdoch certainly wasn't competent. He was called a 'dour Aberdonian' – and much worse in Gaelic. The locals said that Dr Murdoch had learnt his medicine in the days when they sawed off legs with only whisky as an anaesthetic. In the forty years he had practised on the island he had increased the mortality rate among all ages – or so Gille Ruadh said.

One evening he told the story of the English visitor who had been stung by an adder in the south of the island. Dr Murdoch had been phoned, but told the husband that the bite wasn't serious. There would be a small swelling for a few days, and perhaps blurred vision. The woman should take an aspirin and go to bed.

But the visitor had some rare blood condition which made her take an adverse reaction to the adder bite, Gille Ruadh explained to the Maclean family. An hour after she had sat on the snake she was vomiting. Dr Murdoch was phoned again, but couldn't be found.

'The woman died that night,' Gille Ruadh told them before he swallowed more whisky. 'There was an inquest, and Dr Murdoch was criticised for not going to her, but nothing came of it. He was allowed to go on practising. My mother has never gone near him. She says she would rather die (Gille Ruadh used the eloquent Gaelic phrase *B'fhearr leam bàs fhaighinn*) than have him in the house. He's nearly seventy, you know, and getting queerer every day.'

Dr Murdoch was a spiritualist. His wife was dead, but he kept the front seat of his Austin clear for her, and while giving lifts to locals, had been known to converse with her. Some evenings his vehicle could be seen in lonely glens. There was no sign of the doctor, and it was said that he was literally away with the fairies.

'Why doesn't the Health Board retire the old fool and put in a properly qualified doctor trained in modern medicine?' the banker wanted to know.

'Because he doesn't have to retire and anyway, it would be difficult for them to find a replacement,' Gille Ruadh pointed out.

'This is a beautiful island. I'm sure some young doctor would like to come here with his family,' Archie suggested.

The visitor looked at his hostess. He knew her opinion of the island, so he changed the subject and talked about the impending Games.

Where was the Licentiate in Medicine that afternoon that Marsaili was brought down from the school with stomach pains by Cairistiona Bonelli? Not that Alice wanted to call him. She shared her husband's opinion of Dr Murdoch's professional skills. One evening, when she was up in the surgery, seeing him about another matter, he noticed the small mole growing on her face and suggested that he could easily remove it in his surgery, using a scalpel and local anaesthetic. The thought of letting the Licentiate loose on her features with a blade made Alice feel ill. She told him politely that she had lived with the mole for many years, and hoped it would be with her till the end.

That blustery afternoon when her daughter was brought home from school Alice blamed the crabs which had been handed in by one of the banker's customers. However, he pointed out that they had all eaten them for supper, and that Marsaili was the only one of the family who was unwell.

Alice gave her daughter two aspirins and helped her up to bed. But when she was working in the kitchen, she heard her moaning above, so she went down the stairs to her husband's office.

'We need to get Dr Murdoch.'

'That's a pity,' her husband said, picking up the phone. 'Do you happen to know where Dr Death is today?' he asked Gille Ruadh, who was on duty while his mother was having her nap. 'Marsaili has a sore stomach.'

Gille Ruadh informed the banker that the Doctor was answering a call down the island.

'I'll leave a message,' the operator said.

This was a day in January, with the wind strengthening throughout the brief hours of daylight, the time of year that Alice hated. Burns Night had passed, and it was a long haul to the summer through a winter of severe gales, buffeted windows, seaweed strewn on Main Street, the contents of her bin scattered. At such times the bank manager's wife wished that she lived in a warm climate, like Spain. Some hope. There was no Gaelic in that distant country, and her husband would hardly take a day trip to the mainland.

By the time the faces of the town clock were lighting the darkness Marsaili was crying with the pain in her abdomen, and the angry banker was on the phone to the doctor, just back from down the island.

The wind is rising and Alice's nerves are in shreds. She is

smoking and going through the house, lamenting, 'oh why did we come to this bloody island? That poor girl upstairs is in such pain, yet that fool of a doctor's been down the island, talking to fairies instead of attending to his patients.' She rounded on her husband. 'I hope you'll write to the Health Board and get him retired. Because if you don't, I will. I'll tell them what I've had to go through today.'

Marsaili shouted for a basin to be brought up, but was sick before her mother could reach her. The doorbell rang and Dr Murdoch came up the stairs with a slow heavy tread. He put a thermometer into Marsaili's mouth and stood at the window while waiting for the reading.

'What is it?' Alice asked fearfully.

He took her arm and led her out of the room.

'It's her period.'

'Her period?' Alice said incredulously. 'She's been having her period for a year and has never been ill like this. Headaches and pains, yes, not vomiting.'

'That's what it is, Mrs Maclean. Do you have any Milk of Magnesia in the house? If not send one of your boys to the chemist's for a bottle. That will settle her.'

Marsaili immediately brought up the spoonful of the white paste on to her quilt. Her mother goes down to the bank and demands that her husband come up instantly.

'Her period?' she repeated, furious, as they stood in the doorway to their daughter's room. 'If you don't phone that old fool and get him to come back down here right away, I'm going up to his house.'

Dr Murdoch is back down within ten minutes, having left his glass of whisky and the paper he is writing on fairies in the Hebrides for an esoteric journal to which he subscribes. This time he pronounces that Marsaili has appendicitis.

Alice has hysterics and her husband is very angry.

'Why didn't you diagnose this sooner, Kenneth?'

'Appendicitis,' he repeats, as if he hasn't heard the banker. 'The lassie's going to have to be taken to the mainland.'

'In *this* weather?' Archie says incredulously.

'I'll use your phone to arrange a boat.'

The banker goes downstairs to phone Gille Ruadh. They have the ship-to-shore service on in the exchange, and the skipper of a trawler is calling for assistance because of the atrocious weather. But Gille Ruadh doesn't tell his friend and patron this.

'They'll get her to the mainland,' he reassures the banker. He doesn't tell Archie that five years before he came to the island, a woman from the Ross died in the ambulance on her way to the ferry because of Dr Murdoch's procrastination.

When he passes on Gille Ruadh's opinion to his wife Archie is answered with a tirade.

'If this turns out all right, then you're asking for a shift to the mainland,' she informs him. 'And if you don't you'll be staying here alone.'

Angus the lobster fisherman comes up the stairs in his stockinged feet, his long seaboots left in the stairwell below. In view of the wildness of the night, he tells the banker in Gaelic, they are going to take the ferry-boat that plies across the sound. It's a converted wartime vessel and can withstand heavy seas.

'Alasdair MacTavish will skipper it.'

The accordionist has been about boats since he was a child and is probably the best seaman on the island. Every August he participates in the Regatta, a thirty mile race down the sound. It's a thrilling sight to stand on the terrace of the Hebridean Hotel and watch his Dragon coming round the headland, with the crew lying out, and Alasdair in blue oilskins at the tiller. He's always up there, among the winners.

By now Alice is raging that she will be writing to the Prime Minister about incompetent island doctors, and also the lack of suitable hospital facilities. Marsaili hears her mother's voice as she is lifted on to the stretcher and carried carefully down the winding stairs. Outside, her mother uses her body to shield her daughter from the blast. The sea is throwing spray in their faces, soaking the stretcher as they go towards the slipway where the ferry-boat is waiting, its engine running.

Even before they leave the bay the launch is pitching. Alice has been silenced by sickness, and her husband is beside Alasdair at the wheel, talking in Gaelic to keep his mind occupied. This is a night the Maclean family wish never to repeat in the sound where they have travelled so often on the steamer. It is exceptional and terrifying, the way the launch is rolling, as if it will capsize.

Mairi, the district nurse, is travelling with the patient. Off the lighthouse Marsaili is in such pain that the nurse gives her an injection of morphine. It shocks Alice out of her own sickness. She keeps shouting to Alasdair to make the boat go faster, but there is no more power left in the engines.

Marsaili is beyond pain now, in another realm. This is when she notices, through the opened door, the figure standing beside Alasdair MacTavish. He wasn't there when she was carried aboard. She can't see his face, but he's leaning over, touching the wheel between Alasdair's hands. The accordionist doesn't seem to know of his presence, but he's very real to Marsaili, in his long coat and sou'wester.

An ambulance was parked on the pier with its doors pinned open, and the surgeon was waiting in his white smock and white boots up at the Cottage Hospital, the instruments laid out. After two hours the surgeon emerged.

'It was touch and go,' he told Marsaili's parents, who were sitting holding hands. 'Her appendix had burst. Another half an hour and I couldn't have saved her.'

Alice stayed with her daughter for the fortnight she was in hospital and Archie, who could barely boil a kettle, had to get his meals sent along from the Arms. He ratcheted a sheet of paper into his typewriter and punched out a letter to the Health Board. In view of the fact that his daughter had almost died through the 'inexcusable delay in Dr Murdoch's diagnosis of her true condition,' wasn't it time that the Licentiate was retired, to spend even more time communing with the fairies?

Three months later Dr Murdoch announced that he was retiring, and at a presentation in the hall he was given a cheque for £500 and books of his choosing, all to do with the afterlife.

'We should have sued the old fool,' Alice told her family.

It would be years before Marsaili told her father about the spectral figure she had seen on the launch that night she had been taken to hospital. Archie asked Gille Ruadh about it on the phone, and next night, when he was up in the house, he asked Marsaili for a description of the figure. Was he wearing oilskins? No, it didn't look like oilskins, more like cloth. How long was the coat? Almost down to his heels.

'You saw Calum Mor MacAskill,' Gille Ruadh told her.

This was a name that had never come up in conversation before, so the banker pressed their visitor for an explanation.

'He was skipper on that boat in the wartime, until the accident. He always wore a long Ulster coat.'

The banker gave Gille Ruadh time to have a swallow of whisky. It was going to be a good story, and mustn't be spoiled by rushing.

One evening towards the end of the war a torpedo boat had come round the headland in atrocious visibility and collided with the launch. Calum Mor was thrown through the window and killed.

'The strange thing is, they never recovered the body,' Gille Ruadh continued. 'It must have been swept out to sea.'

'Why would I see him?' Marsaili asked.

'You weren't the first,' the visitor informed her. 'Several people who were taken to hospital in that same boat reported seeing him, helping at the wheel. It's strange, but the crew have never seen him.'

'I don't believe in that kind of thing,' Alice said as she broke open her gift of Black Magic, offering her daughter first choice. 'That's what put that old fool Murdoch off his head.'

22.
The Discs of the Dead

Miss MacLaren's coffin came off the same boat as the new jukebox for the Sea Breezes Café, both wrapped in sacking, both treated with equal respect. By the next afternoon Marsaili was sitting by the illuminated machine in the whitewashed coolness of the café – an old fisherman's store – as a Jim Reeves single was swung on to the turntable, and 'I love you because. . .' went out onto Main Street where passers-by stopped to listen. That same afternoon Miss MacLaren, now in her coffin, was taken down to the church in MacPhail's hearse, and when Marsaili went for a walk with her friends round the top of the town when the café closed, there was a moon over the bay, and boards round the MacLaren family layer in the cemetery.

'Come here, Marsaili,' her father had said one pouring wet afternoon, calling her across to the window of their sitting-room. He put an arm round her shoulders. 'You see that old woman down there with the basket on her arm? That's Miss MacLaren. Look at the way her shoes are broken at the back. And her coat's all ragged at the sleeves. She's going into Joey's to ask for two sausages on credit till she gets her pension on Thursday, and of course he'll give them to her for nothing out of the goodness of his heart. What he doesn't know is that she has fifty thousand in deposit in my bank downstairs, and she's in every second day, asking about the interest.'

'Where did she get all that money?' Marsaili asked in wonder.

'She had three uncles, who had their own crofts, which she inherited. They were worth hardly anything till the car ferry came and people wanted ground to build holiday homes. Miss MacLaren got the ground decrofted and sold it as plots. She was one of the few native Gaelic speakers left in the town, and people felt that she should have held on to the crofts, to preserve something of the old way of life.'

Marsaili saw Miss MacLaren once after that conversation, in the Co-op. She was staring at a wedge of cheese on a shelf, and when Neil the manager passed he dropped it into her basket and told her not to go near the check-out. She was three days dead in her house before Andy the postman forced the door.

'That was Nicol the lawyer on the phone,' Archie Maclean informed his family at supper on the day the jukebox had been installed. Marsaili was unable to eat her lobster because she had fallen in love with Jim Reeves, a passion that had turned to tears because of his tragic end in a plane crash which she had been reading about in one of her sister's magazines. Evidently he had left a stack of recorded songs, so he was continuing to sing to the world from beyond the grave.

'Miss MacLaren has made me her executor,' the banker announced.

His wife gave him that look when she was uncertain about something.

'It's not good news, Alice. I have to go up to her house tonight to look for a will because there's all that money in the bank, and the house as well.'

'Has she any relatives?' Alice asked.

'She never spoke about any. Marsaili, if you could tear yourself away from the new jukebox, perhaps you'd come up and help me search. Put on your oldest clothes.'

Marsaili resented losing an evening with Jim Reeves and her friends in the café, but she went up the brae with her father. In these days you didn't need to lock your front door and besides, who would go into such a place? They met the sour smell at the threshold, and it got worse as they turned into the small front room with ashes in the fireplace, and the paper peeling off the speckled wall under the window. The kitchen was only a lean-to at the back, with a chipped stone sink full of pots piled in with dozens of pieces of china, and a frying pan with the scoop submerged in solidified fat. Marsaili opened the door of the toilet and saw sulphur-coloured mushrooms on the wall.

'What a way to live,' the banker said sadly. 'And she had so much money. She could have paid her way in Sunset Court and had all her comforts. All that money in my bank, and for what? I've seen it so often since I've come to the island, this acquisitiveness when they've got so much – far more than will see out their days. Old Jessie sat by her sister's bed for three days and nights, feeding her beef tea so that she would revive for long enough to change her will. Jessie was worth thirty thousand already, and so mean that she took food from her neighbours rather than buy it herself. This is a strange island, Marsaili, so beautiful, with such good Gaelic, but full of such strange people.'

Marsaili helped her father to go through Miss MacLaren's boxes and drawers. They turned out packets of snapshots, showing her standing by the railing.

'She was a good-looking woman,' the banker mused. 'I wonder why she never married.'

They went up the narrow staircase, into a bedroom. The old spinster had obviously been sleeping on the stained horsehair mattress under the pile of old coats, skeins of stockings and knickers strewn among broken shoes on the floorboards, as if she had put up a desperate fight for her honour against an intruder.

'It's disgusting,' Marsaili protested.

'She was an old woman, living by herself,' her father said factually.

'You'll need a lot of sacks to clear this mess,' Marsaili warned him.

'I'll get someone with a van to take the stuff up to the dump. But as her executor I have to go through the place in case there's money lying about. When Donnie the blacksmith died I found over a thousand pounds in his house, and War Bonds too. I wouldn't think there's anything in here, though, because money under the bed doesn't gather interest, and Miss MacLaren was obsessed with interest. I'd better look in here before we go,' he said, turning the handle of the door across the small landing.

It was as if they had stepped through the wall into another house. The room was neat and smelt of polish. The bed was made, with a blue cover, and white sheets turned down over it. There was a polished brass telescope lying at the window overlooking the bay, the fresh-looking floral curtains held back on hooks. Marsaili opened the wardrobe and saw a dark uniform with gold braid hanging up.

'Don't tell me that Miss MacLaren had a secret love,' the banker said. 'Well, well, I'm always learning, though sometimes it's a shock.'

'That must be him,' Marsaili pointed to a photograph on the wall.

A handsome man in a naval uniform and white starched collar was standing with a braided cap pressed between his arm and his side.

The banker lifted the photograph off the wall.

'We'll take it down and show Gille Ruadh tonight. He'll tell us who Miss MacLaren's secret lover was.'

Gille Ruadh glanced at the photograph Marsaili held in front of him.

'That's her brother Murdo. He worked in the store at the pier until someone – it may have been Murchison the minister – got him a bursary to go to nautical college. He did very well and was a captain by the outbreak of the war.'

'What happened to him?' the banker asked.

'He was home on leave from the navy when a cargo boat was driven on to Hound Point in the worst storm I can remember. Murdo went out on the lifeboat, but it capsized. His sister was never the same after that. They were very close, you see, and she was so proud of how well he had done at sea. She went queer after that.'

'Murdo's picture will have to go to the dump with the rest of the stuff – unless the museum would like it,' the banker had a sudden idea.

'If the museum had pictures of all the men who've been lost at sea from this place, there wouldn't be space for anything else,' Gille Ruadh said abruptly.

The next night Marsaili and her father took the picture back up to Miss MacLaren's hovel. Marsaili pulled open a drawer and lifted out a pile of starched collars, neatly tied together. She tried one on in front of the mirror and wondered if she could create a new fashion among her own generation, but decided against it. The drawer below contained long-johns that had been ironed and folded by loving hands, with fragrant little sachets of lavender left to deter moths.

'She must have loved her brother very much to keep his room as a shrine,' the banker said. 'It shows how little we know about people.'

'Look at this,' Marsaili said.

There was an old-fashioned gramophone with a horn – the

kind you see in old books, with a dog sitting listening – on a table in a corner, a pile of old records beside it. The banker slid a disc reverently from its brown paper sleeve and held it up at the window. 'There's not a scratch on it,' he said. 'It's a collector's item.'

Marsaili was bored, thinking of the new jukebox in the Sea Breezes Café. It had an illuminated panel, and an arm passed with a click across the record before the stylus was lowered and Jim Reeves's voice made her tremble. Marsaili hated that old house with its reeking clothes and stiff collars of the dead. She wanted down to the new sound, the flashing lights, friends of her own age.

'No one will want this,' her father said, putting his hand on the lid of the gramophone, as if he were blessing it. 'Everything's electric now.' He started to wind the handle at the side, then opened the lid and lowered the record on to the spindle. There was a hissing sound, and then a man started singing.

'That's Neil Maclean,' he told his daughter. 'I heard him once in the St Andrews Halls in Glasgow before the war. It was a huge place, but he didn't need to use a microphone.'

Marsaili was thinking, the arm will be coming out on the jukebox in the Sea Breezes Café, selecting another record on the lit console, and my friends will be clapping, and I am here, among the brittle discs of the dead, with the drowned man watching me from the wall.

'What a tragedy, having to put these records to the dump,' the banker said.

'You don't have to send them to the dump,' Marsaili pointed out with the impatience of youth, because there was still time to get down to the café. 'It wouldn't be dishonest if you took them for yourself, because no one else will want them.'

'Can you not hear your mother when we carry them up the stairs and put them beside the record player? When I listen to the Gaelic request programme on the radio she finds an excuse to be at the top of the house.'

He put another record on the turntable. This time it was a woman singing.

'That's Margrat Duncan from Islay,' the banker said. 'She's singing about a boatman, saying she often asks the boat crews if they've seen him, and if he's safe.'

Marsaili understood now. Miss MacLaren must have climbed the stairs from the shambles below and sat listening to the record, thinking about her brother, keeping him afloat in her memory. The song about the boatman was even more haunting than the Jim Reeves number that had kept her awake the night before. It seemed to get into her bones, making her tingle.

'I'll take the records,' Marsaili told her father.

'We have to get them into the house, past your mother,' he said conspiratorially. 'We'll find something to carry them in among the junk downstairs.'

'What's that you've got?' Alice enquired as her husband lugged the box up the stairs.

'Something from Miss MacLaren's house that Marsaili wanted.'

'What is it?' Alice asked suspiciously as Marsaili opened the door to her bedroom so that her father could bring in the records.

It's now October. There are white horses in the bay and the hump on Miss MacLaren's grave has greened over. Marsaili's friends don't go to the Sea Breezes Café in the evenings because the new batch of records – including the latest Jim Reeves – has failed to arrive. She has worn down the grooves of the old 78 record playing *Fear a' Bhàta*, to her mother's annoyance.

> *'S tric mi sealltuinn o'n chnòc a's àirde*
> *Dh'fheuch am faic mi fear a bhàta*
> I climb the mountain and scan the ocean
> For thee, my boatman, with fond devotion. . .

23.
Home Movies

When Archie Maclean retired from the bank Alice wanted them to
move back to the mainland, to buy a house on the hill in the town
where they were both born. But he refused to leave the island,
saying that there was no Gaelic left on the mainland and anyway,
he had been away for so long, he didn't know anyone.

Alice had her eye on the old Baptist manse at the top of the
town, but her husband insisted on buying a flat on Main Street,
even though it was two flights up. It wasn't to stop her having to
lug bags of shopping up the brae to the manse. He wanted a home
where people could come up to visit him when they were down
on Main Street.

So locals with Gaelic made their way up the turnpike stairs in
the old tenement, where fisher families had once lived in
overcrowded conditions The banker presided in that room with
coomed ceilings overlooking the bay, listening to their stories and

songs, and also dispensing drams. Alice brought in the tea tray for the visitors, then retired next door, to the dining-room, to read until they had gone. When Marsaili phoned from Glasgow, her mother complained at the constant intrusion.

'I'm sick of the sound of Gaelic. You would think there was nothing else in life. I want to come to Glasgow for a week, to see you, but your father won't move, as if he's frightened of missing something when he's away. Marsaili will be home soon, he says. Well, I tell him, you're lucky having such a dutiful daughter who also happens to love this place. God knows why. It's even windier in this house than it was in the bank house. Why did they build them so high?'

The banker got even more eccentric in his habits. He would lie awake long into the night, reading the Gaelic Bible, not because he had become religious, but because of the beauty of the language. Whenever he came across a word he didn't know he reached under the bed for an old Gaelic dictionary that Gille Ruadh had presented him with.

Major James (Jamie) Farquhar continued to visit him, climbing the stairs in wellington boots, complaining when he eventually reached the top that his knees were 'buggered' after all those years of this damp island. He sat opposite his hostess, his kilted legs planted wide until she was forced to excuse herself and go next door.

'You've been here a long time, Jamie,' his former banker prompted him.

'Over thirty years?'

'But you're happy here,' his host said reassuringly.

'You know, Archie, some nights I wake up and ask myself, why didn't I take another day in Italy to attend to the Countess? Why was I in such a hurry to get home, when I've made such a mess of things?'

Archie Maclean had heard such cries when he was in the bank.

People who had arrived on the island with substantial balances found themselves with large overdrafts after a few years. Where had all their assets gone? Having soothed them with a dram, the banker hinted that they might have trusted the locals too much. All he could offer the Major in consolation was more whisky from the bottle which the visitor would finish before he was ready to go home, and then he had a request.

'Would you help me down to the car?' he would ask the banker, and Archie would go down in front in case the decorated officer who had led his men through the labyrinth of Monte Cassino's ruins fell head-first down the stairs. When they reached the street the retired banker would open the door of his former customer's Land Rover, then plant one wellington boot on the clutch, the other on the brake.

When the banker climbed back up he found his wife had put the empty whisky bottle into the kitchen bin.

'Why doesn't he wear something under that kilt?' she complained vehemently.

'Because he's an old soldier,' her husband replied with a smile, picturing the receptive Countess in the ruins of her villa.

The banker's bones were stiffening on the stairs, and there were days when he didn't go down. The window was at too awkward an angle to allow him to continue filming the activity on Main Street, and besides, so many of the worthies were now dead. His collection was now an archive, as much part of the history of the town as the museum. So Alice, and any member of the family who happened to be at home, had to sit through impromptu showings in which the dead, many of them drunk, staggered across the white wall while the film-maker chuckled behind the turning reels.

One film he played more than most featured Gille Ruadh up on the Games field, a small flustered-looking man in his too-tight gaberdine suit, the Secretary's rosette wilting in his lapel as the shadow of the toppling caber passed over him. Gille Ruadh waddled over to his tent, and there was an intermission for some Highland dancing till the Secretary reappeared, much refreshed from a bottle. Gille Ruadh had died the previous year, after the exchange had gone automatic. The telephone company had given him a small pension, but he missed living in the lives of others by listening into their calls.

Every week Alice came up the turnpike stairs to tell her husband that there was a new death notice in Black's window, another native Gaelic speaker with marvellous stories carried up to the cemetery. One by one the characters in his epic film died; silent shades wending home from the Arms, which was under new ownership now.

When Marsaili came home she drove her father round the top of the town. He pointed out houses where the people had lived without running water, but with Gaelic so pure, so free flowing that it could only have come from the Creator Himself.

'The language is dying, lassie,' he told his daughter. 'I used to be able to go for most of the day in my office without having to speak much English – except to the white settlers, of course. But I can go for a whole day now without having a conversation in Gaelic.'

'Why is it dying?' his daughter wanted to know.

'You must remember that our language had a very fragile hold on this island and elsewhere, because most people couldn't read or write Gaelic. They could only speak it, so they relied on the oral tradition, and when that began to die, there was nothing else. Then the accursed television came and killed conversation.

'This island is too close to the mainland, Marsaili. That's why it has attracted so many white settlers. They bought estates and houses here and employed the locals, but they didn't want them speaking Gaelic, in case they were miscalling their employers. People had to make an effort to hold on to their Gaelic. Whatever Gille Ruadh might have done – and he did plenty of shady things in his career –

he was at least loyal to his native language. You can forgive a person a great deal if he's like that.'

Marsaili was operating on a golden retriever in her Glasgow surgery when the call came through from the island. Her assistant thought it best not to interrupt her until the animal on the table had been stitched up, and then she came in with the sad news. Her father had died that afternoon. Evidently he had been feeling a tightness in his chest, and after lunch had got up, and to distract himself had threaded 'one of those bloody films' (her mother's expression) through the projector. Gille Ruadh came waddling out of his tent, to see how the piping competition was progressing, but the man behind the turning spools was slumped in his chair.

It was, Marsaili knew, the kind of death that he would have wanted. At least that was what she told herself as she drove north, in the russet magnificence of autumn, with audible streams and mists round the summits of the bens, a day of Gaelic grandeur, if there ever was one. On the ferry an old farmer who had been told of the banker's passing by the crew came forward to hug her, and to tell her in breaking Gaelic how her father had saved him and his family in the hard times of the credit squeeze in the 1960s.

By the time Marsaili had climbed the turnpike stairs, the cine projector had been dismantled, and the district nurse, one of the last Gaelic tradition-bearers in the town, had washed the retired banker and laid him out on his bed. As his daughter stooped to kiss his chilly brow her toe stubbed the Gaelic Bible, open at the Beatitudes.

Alice wanted him taken to the mainland for burial, where he belonged, but Marsaili was backed by her siblings in insisting that he would only lie at peace in the cemetery up the brae, beside Gille Ruadh and the others who had brought him so much pleasure and laughter through their Gaelic stories.

The church couldn't possibly accommodate those who came

from the island, never mind the outlying islands and the mainland as well. It was undoubtedly the largest funeral in living memory – much larger than the laird's. The full-bosomed Mary Ann MacTaggart, who had performed in the banker's summer ceilidhs, sang at his funeral, and there was a Gaelic tribute from an old man who had to be helped on to a chair at the front, beside the coffin. Not more than a dozen people in the packed congregation knew what he was saying.

Two nights later Alice laid out her late husband's effects on the bed and invited their children to choose. That was when Marsaili took the box of films, when Calum suggested that their father's bed be given to the museum, since it didn't have an example of a long-boat.

That bed had been the subject of matrimonial stress and discord for many years. Archie had insisted on bringing it from the mainland, because it had been his parents', though Alice wanted to order an interior sprung bed. As the banker got stouter through the rich food that his clients left for him behind his storm-door, the springs began to sag. When some of them went, the banker asked Murdo the telephone engineer to come up. He repaired them with wire with the same care as if he were re-stringing a priceless harp.

Now her husband was dead, Alice could have sent the bed to the dump and ordered a new single one, with special posture springs. But the old one had too many memories for her, and she continued to occupy its declivity despite her rheumatics.

Marsaili missed these long conversations in Gaelic over the phone with her father, while her supper spoiled in the oven in her Glasgow home. She had a new bulb put into the projector, and relived her childhood on the wall of her dining-room. Alice's phone calls were litanies of complaint about the weather, the fact that she now knew hardly anyone in the town. Marsaili and Douglas had several serious conversations before Alice was invited to come and live with them, but she refused, implying on the bad line that she preferred to die a martyr on the island, brained by a slate on Main Street.

Every Thursday morning Marsaili parked on double yellow lines outside the newsagent's on Byres Road to pick up the paper that her mother used to send her down to the shop for, as soon as the steamer came in. Before she began the day's work in her surgery she read the death notices over a cup of coffee.

> *Major James (Jamie) Farquhar, formerly of the London*
> *Scottish and Black Watch. Peacefully, at his home. . .*

Alice had the sad story on the phone that evening. The Major had developed dementia. Every time he heard a rumble of thunder he threw himself to the floor, believing that he was back at Monte Cassino and that the Germans were launching another offensive. One evening the ordinary staircase in his Georgian home had turned into a gilded extravaganza. The figure standing on it wasn't his long-suffering wife, coaxing him to take his pills, but the Countess, still in the radiance of her beauty, beckoning him up to her bombed apartments with a crooked finger.

He began to hear rats that had long since been poisoned by the pilchards of the former mine-layer. He began to hear the voices of children in his garden, though his own, and his wife's, were adults now. One morning, coming down the stairs, he forgot to put on his moth-eaten London Scottish kilt, and the daily from the village left, calling him a 'dirty brute'.

In his distress the Major didn't take one of his pair of Holland and Holland guns from his cupboard. He was a soldier, after all. Since coming to the island he had fought an invasion of rats, escaping mink, moles sabotaging his daffodils. He had waited patiently for his stern mother to die in her hotel suite in Harrogate, where she had been taking the waters for forty years.

The Major was found wandering naked on the road at 2am,

insisting that he was on a secret mission to blow 'those bastards out of the monastery.' He was taken to the same asylum on the mainland where Muldonaich had received electric shock treatment for having molested a Halloween guiser who later changed her story.

The Major died of exhaustion, a man who had fought too many battles, against Germans and moles. Marsaili smiled at the recollection of the holed kilt, the wellingtons that had to be placed on clutch and brake pedals so that he could get home.

Later, when his obituary appeared in the local paper, written by one of his own class, she noticed that the Major had been cremated on the mainland, but that his ashes had been brought back to the island and scattered in the lonely glen where he had learned to shoot roding woodcock as a boy.

A year after his death, Archie Maclean got a headstone, a handsome Iona cross paid for by his children, including Marsaili. There was a lot of discussion over the inscription. Marsaili wanted it all to be in Gaelic, including the rendering of his name, as if to show the special bond of language that had been between herself and her parent.

She was outvoted by her siblings. However, as a concession, she was allowed to choose a Gaelic expression for the stone. She kept the mason waiting for a month while she consulted books and her father's few surviving Gaelic-speaking friends in the town. She found appropriate lines in an elegy by Sorley MacLean.

> *Thuig iad doimhne throm do dhaondachd*
> *Nuair a b' aotroime do spòrs*
> They understood the heavy depths of your humanity
> when your fun was at its lightest

24.
Guest of Honour

Marsaili Henderson stopped her car on double yellow lines to buy a bunch of red roses from the stall in the alcove by the library. She knew she could get more lasting ones in the florist's across the road, but she felt sorry for the little Asian with the soulful eyes who got up to go to the fruit market for these sad blooms after the shops have had their pick. She left him the change.

As she crossed the road she saw the traffic warden beside her vehicle. But he didn't have his ticket book out. His hand was in the gap of her open back window, and her black labrador was licking his fingers.

'She's a beauty,' he said.

'She's old now.'

'I had to have my own dog put down last year,' he told her sorrowfully.

She didn't tell him that she was a vet and that putting animals to sleep was part of her duties, and that it was not always heartbreaking if they were very sick. She laid the flowers on the back seat and drove home to her stone villa, with an extension for servants, in the notable terrace beside the Botanic Gardens in Glasgow. The flowers are an annual ritual for Douglas. As she arranges them in the vase in the kitchen she can hardly believe that it's three years. She carries the vase through to the sitting-room and places it on the shelf.

Douglas died at the age of forty-eight on the squash court. He hadn't been pushing himself. In fact he was practising, waiting for his partner, who was fifteen minutes late because of traffic congestion. By the time the paramedics had shouldered in the resuscitation equipment it was too late. Douglas had crawled up to the glass wall, trying to attract help, his nails dug into the squash ball in his fist because of the agony in his heart.

Marsaili lifts down the brass compass from the shelf beside the flowers and carries it to the armchair. It's as if she's cradling his dear head in her lap. It holds so many memories for her. Spray is misting the glass as they speed up the sound, with the spinnaker bellying above in the blue sky. They are out front in their class in the Regatta. She's at the helm and Douglas is scrambling in the cockpit, ropes snaking through the winches.

Another evening, the glass of the compass is clear, and there's no race on. They have taken hours to tack up the sound, and now they are turning into the bay of her home town. As Douglas gets ready to drop the sails she looks at the rock they are passing beside the pier. The story is that a family were caught in a terrific gale out in the Atlantic. With their mainsail in tatters they somehow battled into the bay, one of the most sheltered anchorages on the west coast. The father bought a tin of whitewash and a brush in Black's. He steered his dinghy under the rock and painted in large white letters: JESUS WILL SAVE YOU. The Baptists kept the letters fresh every year, but their church closed and as the boat passes fifty yards from the rock, Marsaili can't read the promise.

stories from an island   191

The mainsail is fluttering down now. Ahead is the granite tower of the four-faced clock. The anchor chain is slithering out as Douglas finds a space among the boats. There must be ninety in the bay tonight.

'The Maxtons are in,' he says, pointing to the conspicuous yacht anchored across at the waterfall. The plan is that they will go across to their boat, before they all go up to supper, to the Hebridean Hotel above the pier, where they have a table booked for four.

Douglas has gone up to arrange for the wines (it will be a seafood night) to be chilled. Marsaili is feeling wistful. As she looks at the lighted face of the memorial clock floating in the darkening water she is a girl again, sitting with her friends on the stone seat under the clock, hoping to attract local boys as they come down from the golf course with their clutch of clubs in the dusk. Marsaili's eyes move along Main Street to the bank house, where a stranger now occupies her room.

A yacht comes into the bay, its sails flapping as they are lowered by two ghostly figures at the boom. She wonders where they have come from because there is always something romantic about a sail-boat arriving. The memory she cherishes most is of going round the Mull of Kintyre at midnight, with the pulse of the lighthouse on Douglas's face as he stood at the tiller. At that moment she realised how precious he was to her.

A shout intrudes into her memory.

'Is there a vet about?' someone calls across the bay.

'Here!' she calls back spontaneously, though she is on holiday.

'Can you come over here?'

But Douglas is away with the rubber dinghy, and they have to send a boat across for her. She expects to find a sick dog. She is critical of those who take their pets on boats, because animals as well as humans can get sea-sick and besides, they need room to roam. She climbs down into the cockpit.

'It's over here,' the man says.

At first sight Marsaili thinks it's a joke, a soft toy. The puffin is lying on its side on a table.

'Where did you get this?' she says angrily, because there is a law about taking wild birds.

'It fell on the deck when we were coming past the Holy Isles last night.'

Marsaili has treated parrots and cockatoos before, and has had a macaw curse her as she bound its injured foot, but she has never had to attend a seabird. Is it a wing? She spreads them out, but she sees no damage. She opens the gorgeous bill, but there is no sign of blood, and no bruise on the head. The question is, is this bird dead? Certainly its eye looks glassy. She runs a finger into the white down on the breast and locates a tiny beat, but it may be her own anxious heart.

The man looks at her, expecting her to do something. She can tell him to take it ashore to George MacIsaac the vet, but she suspects that he will be just as wise about puffins as she is.

'I'll see what I can do,' she tells the man, picking up the bird. She carries it in the crook of her arm like a newborn baby as he helps her into the rubber dinghy. It swerves between the anchored yachts as it takes her back to their own boat. It's now seven. The meal with the Maxtons is at eight. She has some quick thinking to do. She should wash and get changed. Instead she asks the man, 'Could you put me ashore, please?' and he takes her to the steps where half a dozen dinghies are tethered, their owners singing along with the accordion in the Ceilidh Bar.

Marsaili walks along Main Street and pushes the button on the lit intercom box, and her mother's crackling voice wants to know who is calling. Alice is two up in the flat she has lived in since her husband retired from the bank, and will not move despite the steep winding stairs. 'I have the memories of your father here,' she has often told Marsaili.

'What have you got there?' her mother asks suspiciously.

'A puffin.'

Alice recoils. She has never been able to come to terms with creatures from the sea. When grateful customers left a pail of lobsters behind the storm door at the foot of the stairs because their bank manager had sorted their tax, she complained that they shrieked as she plunged them into boiling water. Under cover of darkness she sent her children down to the shore below the house, to cut the string round their claws and release them back into the sea.

'Where are father's books?' Marsaili asks.

'Are you going to take them at last?' her mother says thankfully. Ever since his death she has been on at their daughter to take his Gaelic books – mostly dictionaries – out of her way, though she is living alone in a five apartment house.

'Not just now, mother. I want to look up something.'

She leaves the puffin lying on a cushion on the sofa –her mother won't go near it – and goes to the shelf for a bird book. She reads about the life cycle of the puffin, but there are no instructions on how to treat a sick one. Then she plucks one of her father's well-used Gaelic dictionaries from the shelf and looks up the word for puffin. *Peata ruadh*, red pet.

'Do you have a shoe box, mother?'

This entails clearing wallets of family photographs from a box in the sideboard. Her mother has a photograph of her husband at a Burns Supper, and wants to reminisce about his wit and eloquence when delivering the Immortal Memory, but Marsaili is very short of time. She lines the box with kitchen roll and lays the puffin in. She's no nearer deciding what to do.

At seven forty five she leaves the house with the puffin in the box under her arm, with her mother conversing with the dead in the photographs scattered on the sofa. Marsaili should go out to the boat to change, but there isn't time. Their guests will have to take her as she is. She cradles the box in her arms as she goes round the swing doors in the hotel. The receptionist comes round from her desk, thinking that Marsaili is making a delivery of posies for a wedding the next day. Douglas and the Maxtons are waiting for her in the conservatory above the sea, the bay below bright with the lights of yachts, and beyond, the dark calm sound.

'What kept you?' Douglas asks, taking her aside. 'We've been here for half an hour.'

'An emergency, dear.'

'Is there something wrong with the boat?' he asks anxiously.

'The boat's fine.'

'I thought you were putting on your new dress.'

'I didn't have time. I'll explain later,' she promises her spouse.

'What's in the box?' he enquires tersely. Douglas is the type of man who worries about details and wants everything right.

'Later, dear,' she says, laying her hand soothingly on his arm.

They follow the waiter to the dining-room, where they have a table in the bay window. There are flowers in a vase, and name cards arranged by Douglas. Marsaili puts the box down by the scuffed blue canvas shoes she should have changed out of. Their guests are talking about their day's sail.

'We've got one of these automatic rudders. It's wonderful,' Bill enthuses. 'You set it and don't have to worry about a thing. Go below for a couple of hours and when you come up, you're still on course. We used it last week to cross to Barra.'

'We must get one,' Douglas turns to Marsaili.

Marsaili lifts up the box and removes the lid.

'Your rudder's not as wonderful as this little fellow,' she tells the company.

They lean over, looking at the bird lying in its bed of paper.

'It's a puffin,' Wendy Maxton says. They are not into birds, though they sail the west coast for a month every summer. But they have seen puffins whirring past, like brightly painted clockwork toys about to crash into the sea.

'This little fellow was about to migrate when he flew smack into a yacht and was left behind by the others.' Marsaili got this information from her father's bird book. 'They fly across the Atlantic in early August and drift about in rafts among the icebergs for the winter. Can you imagine what that means?' She turns to their guests, and Wendy shakes her head at this impromptu geography lesson.

'This little fellow' – Marsaili strokes its breast with a finger – 'probably spent last spring drifting over the place where the Titanic went down. *Peata ruadh*,' she says, as if trying to soothe it to sleep.

'What did you call it?' Wendy asks.

'Red pet. It's Gaelic for a puffin.'

'I love it,' Wendy says.

'Put that away,' Douglas tells his wife as the waiter arrives to take their order. Marsaili will have sardines for starters.

Wendy leans over and touches the puffin's white breast. 'Go on with what you were saying, Marsaili,' she says in an affected voice.

'You were saying how wonderful your automatic rudder was. But how does a puffin find its way back at the beginning of summer to a burrow on the Holy Isles? Is it navigating by the stars? Following a magnetic field? Who knows, but it gets there – or at least, the others will, because this little fellow has been left behind.'

Their starters arrive and Marsaili dangles a sardine in front of the bird in the box on her knee. 'Come on, *peata ruadh*.' But it won't open its bill.

'Its chick has probably flown with the other birds,' Marsaili says.

'This is very sad,' Wendy says, close to tears.

Marsaili puts a finger into the white down on the bird's breast. 'He probably passed away when we were eating our starter.'

Other diners have left their courses and are crowding round their table, making sorrowful noises. A woman's hand comes out and strokes the white breast. A child is sobbing at his father's back.

'What are you going to do with it?' Douglas asks uneasily. This is not the way he planned the evening. They were to have five courses, lobster with chilled wine, and then they would retire to the conservatory, for Calvados and cigars. In the morning he would take the rubber dinghy out to the Maxtons' boat, and they would agree the lucrative contract.

Marsaili has put the lid on the box, placing it back at her feet, and breaks up the lobster claws in her hands.

'Waste not, want not,' she says.

They eat, but the evening is subdued, and when they go through to the conservatory, Douglas and Bill Maxton step out on to the terrace.

Marsaili goes down the brae with the shoe box under an arm, her other arm through Douglas's.

'I've got the contract,' Douglas says gleefully. 'I was edgy at the beginning, but somehow he seemed to soften.'

On the way back to their yacht the bay is sheened by mast lights and either someone is playing a tin whistle or it is a tune out of Marsaili's imagination when she was a girl here, and the local tinker used to sit under the memorial clock, charming tourists with a selection of Gaelic airs.

Before she climbs the ladder to the deck she opens the box and lays the puffin reverently in the dark tide that is running west.

25.
Conversion

Marsaili was phoned by George MacIsaac's wife to say that he had taken a stroke. His arm sheathed in the waterproof sleeve had been up the cow's vulva when suddenly he had no feeling in his fingers for the calf he was trying to save. His left arm was paralysed, and he wouldn't be able to go back to work. They wanted to sell the practice. Was Marsaili interested?

She stood in the hall of her Glasgow house, the receiver in her hand as the caller awaited her answer. As a young student she had been George's assistant for a summer, and she had learned many things from him. Lately she had been wondering if she should retire to the island. But she was only in her early fifties and loved her work in Glasgow. Perhaps in another five years time?

'Are you still there, Marsaili?'

'I'm here Agnes. I wouldn't want to sell up here and move back. But I might be interested in being your locum for a couple of months, to keep the practice going while you find a buyer.'

'That would be wonderful. But what about your own commitments there?'

'Well, my daughter's in with me now. She'll be taking over from me eventually, so maybe it's time to give her a taste of responsibility.'

When Marsaili told her mother that she was coming home for a couple of months, the old woman was over the moon. She had began to dislike living on the island even more because so many of her friends had died, and the storms seemed to be getting worse. (Alice blamed global warning, though she had no knowledge of science or meteorology.)

Marsaili drove north on an autumn afternoon. She pulled into a lay-by while she ate her picnic. Inevitably she thought of Douglas, and the many trips they had made together, usually by boat through the Crinan Canal. Maybe she should have remarried, but no one suitable had come along and besides, she had plenty to do with her family and her practice.

She drives into the big ferry replaced the *Lochspelvie* and that makes constant crossings with tourist cars and articulated trailers of provisions throughout the summer. She goes up the stairs into the saloon of yellow and red plastic. She looks at the lighted board, but decides that she doesn't want to eat anything. She sits at a yellow table with a paper cup of tea and so many memories.

She doesn't recognise any of the other passengers. Maybe it's a mistake, coming back to the island. She would have been better to have stayed in Glasgow with her memories, she's thinking as she drives off the ferry. The road they used to take in her father's first car when they came off the steamer in the old days was single track, and if it were milking time you might have to sit for ten minutes in a lay-by.

Marsaili is passing the place by the sound where the Morrisons' croft was. She and her father would drive down on a summer evening. She's a girl again, eating buttered scones as the old woman tells her father in her exquisite Gaelic stories of how the Fingalian giants had come from Ireland in the time of the white deer, shaping the glens and mountains with their ferocious battles. But the

stories from an island   199

hillsides have been blasted to make way for the new double-width road for the touring buses that come off the ferry regularly in the season. Marsaili is driving over the Morrisons' croft where the corncrake used to call in the fragrant pasture as the old woman stood at her gate, calling '*oidhche mhath!*' as they drove off. The stream where she watched the dipper bobbing on a stone now runs in a culvert under the new road, instead of under a bridge.

Her mother has a hot meal and plenty of questions about whom she met on the boat.

'I hardly recognise anyone in this town now,' the old woman laments. 'It's time I thought of moving to the mainland.'

'You would miss the island, mother.'

'Miss it, when I'm wondering when the windows are going to come in with the storm? I've had many happy days here, Marsaili, but it's all in the past now. I don't know why you bothered to come back.'

'I want to see how things have changed.'

'You don't need to come to live here to find out.'

On her first evening home Marsaili walked up the brae, past the tangle of honeysuckle she used to smell when she went up to the tennis court as a girl. The top of the town was a layout of short streets, named after Victorian royalty. Some of the gardens were cut off from their houses by the road, the soil in them brought across from Ireland as ballast in boats. The houses seemed to be sunk into the ground, with low lintels, as if they had been built for a race of small people. But the coffins of the owners had long since been carried out of them, and most of them were modernised, holiday homes with double-glazing, shut up for most of the year when local couples were living in caravans with their babies. The gardens where vegetables had been grown had been slabbed.

Marsaili pushes open the gate of the cemetery on the slope at the top of the town and walks up the gravel path to her father's grave. She stands there, thinking about how much he loved life, with the house resounding with laughter and Gaelic songs late into the summer nights.

The vet's surgery was at the top of the town, in the bottom flat of an old house. But Marsaili knew that this practice was very different from her own in the city. She would have to answer calls for help throughout the island at all times of day and night, as she had done as a student. How often had she sat in George's freezing Land Rover, jolting down a track to a sick cow, its recovery vital to the economy of the croft. George never complained that they should have called him out at a more reasonable hour as he pulled on his overalls and wellingtons. Marsaili learned from him that you had to use your back as well as your brains, and that there were conditions that weren't in the textbooks.

Marsaili looked back wistfully to these days when she was a student. She had impromptu Gaelic lessons in the December byre as George laboured to save the foal of one of the last working Clydesdales on the island, the bloody waters breaking. After the successful delivery there was the bliss of a basin of hot water, and then home-made cheese and oatcakes by the Aga in the kitchen.

Marsaili's first call as the island locum was out to a farm in the south of the island. The Macleans were relatives of her father's, and she had been there several times with George. But Sandy Maclean's son wasn't interested in farming. He had left the island to work as an engineer, and when the old man died, the estate had put the farm on the market. It had been bought by a man with a double-barrelled name who had made his fortune in futures on the London exchange.

Marsaili thought she was at the wrong place. The road that had been a rutted track was now tarred, lined with white ranch fencing. The man who came to greet her was wearing a famous brand label on the hip pocket of his denims. He led her through a conservatory into the byre. Marsaili remembered that evening when the herd in their stalls kept up a plaintive lowing that became a wake as George's oilskin-sheathed arm explored the dead life within the distressed mother.

The byre was now living space, with red quarry tiles on the floor. The slit windows had been enlarged to take panoramic panes of double-glazing, and the roof was honey-coloured pine. A woman was sitting on a sumptuous white sofa, sunglasses up on her hair, though it was a gloomy day outside. A poodle was lying beside her on an angora sweater.

'The little darling's off his food,' the woman explained in a tragic voice.

As Marsaili put out her hand to the manicured dog with the silver collar, it snarled.

'She's like that with strangers,' the woman says.

'What's wrong with her?' Marsaili enquires.

'She's been off-colour for the last week, since we came. I thought it was the ferry crossing.'

'Could you hold her while I examine her?' Marsaili asks.

The woman has the hostile animal's head cupped between her hands as Marsaili probes its groomed stomach.

'What are you feeding it?' she asks.

'Her food's sent up from Harrods.'

'Show me, please.'

The man comes back with a small golden tin. Chicken livers.

'How many of these does she get a day?' Marsaili wants to know.

'Three. Don't you darling?' the woman says, hugging the dog.

'It's too rich,' Marsaili tells her. 'Try her on something simpler. How much exercise does she get?'

'I walk her for five minutes in the morning,' the woman says.

'It's not enough,' Marsaili warns. 'Let her out by herself for a run.'

'I couldn't possibly,' the woman says with horror, a cigarette in her mouth as she fiddles with a gas lighter. 'The people in the cottage have a collie. He's always sniffing about her. If she became pregnant by him it would ruin your pedigree, wouldn't it, darling?'

Marsaili realises that this is a lost cause. The poodle will go on stuffing herself with chicken livers. She will have to be carried everywhere, to the manicurist who'll cut her coat in these absurd ruffs at her neck and paws, and maybe even to an animal psychologist because of the stress caused by an overprotective owner.

'How much do we owe you?' the man asks, coming forward with a cheque book.

'I really didn't do anything,' Marsaili says.

But he's scrawling his name in blue ink and handing her a cheque drawn on Coutts. It's for twenty pounds. Marsaili doesn't say, this is too much. She folds the cheque into her bag, to give to George's wife, who looks after the accounts of the practice.

It isn't only the waste of farmland that saddens her as she drives off. Gaelic has gone from this sequestered spot where her father's cousin and his wife spoke nothing else in the house. It's the same all over the island. Farmers tired of struggling on perpetual overdraft have sold out to incomers who have made big killings on the sales of their houses down south. The incomers have torn out the interiors of the buildings and hung batik tapestries on the re-pointed walls. They make candles for the tourists, and some of them are even into stained glass, using figures from what they take to have been Celtic mythology, dreamy-eyed women in off-the-shoulder gowns staring up at the yellow crescent of the moon.

As she drives back to town Marsaili suddenly treads on the brake. There's nothing crossing the road. Suddenly she has the revelation that this is why her father kept the bank house open to all hours on summer nights, with locals welcome to come up off the street. The only gift they needed to bring was Gaelic. They told stories into the small hours, and her father joined in the choruses of the rousing Gaelic songs. She is sitting in a lay-by, with the engine switched off, because she knows now why he did this. Her father knew that he was presiding over the death of his own culture because of the incomers buying up the houses, and the increasing numbers of tourists alighting from the big air-conditioned buses on package deal tours of several islands, with a Scottish show. He wanted to enjoy the last golden age before there were no more feet on the stairs, bringing the treasures of Gaelic.

Even the wildlife seems to have vanished. Where are the hawks that used to flash down the forestry firebreaks when she and her father drove out on a summer evening to the hospitable Morrisons with their Fingalian epics and their bannocks? Where are the eagles swooping down the mountains, the deer bounding across the moor?

Marsaili sits in the lay-by, in the afternoon silence of the island. Its past with its din of battles, its burning garrisons, has gone. What is its future? An ugly stainless steel pipe runs up the gable of a converted farmhouse to take away the smoke from the imported stove. She's glad her father did not live till extreme old age because this would have broken his heart, to hear about a poodle on a white sofa, where Lachie and Phemie had spoken such pure Gaelic.

She is now regretting that she came back. It would have been better to have remained in Glasgow with her memories. Some of them are probably illusions. The light over the bay seemed more intense in those days. The air seemed sharper, purer. Even the sea cleft by the bow of the old mail steamer seemed bluer, more majestic. The insight she has seems to have aged her suddenly, as she sits in the lay-by, watching the empty sky. Suddenly the island feels hostile, as if she doesn't belong here, as if she's no part of its history.

Sometimes, when they were out for a drive, her father would pull into a lay-by and point out to his daughter the subtleties of the landscape. One minute the sun would be shining on the mountain, and then a dark cloud would come from nowhere, making it a depressing, menacing place of rain and ruins.

26.
Sacrificial Site

George's wife phoned after supper to say that a call had come through. Could Marsaili go down tonight and look at a pony? Marsaili thinks that this will be another pet belonging to an incomer, probably bought for a spoiled child.

'Can't it wait till the morning?' her mother asks, because she wants her daughter's company.

But Marsaili doesn't want to sit in on this calm evening, listening to a litany about the weather; how, out there in the Atlantic, another storm is massing to knock out the power supply and to shred her mother's nerves, as if the old gods have it in for this nervous woman who's had to endure the sea for too long.

This time the road under her tyres is a track of exposed stones. As she jolts along she remembers coming to this place several times with her father. He had clients here who were also his friends, fishermen who wove stories in Gaelic as they sat in the sun, making their own lobster creels with wattles and tar.

It had been a settlement of half a dozen houses, built of the stones strewn on the shore, roofed with the timbers that the tide brought in. As the coffins were carried out one by one there had been no new settlers. Ahead she can see the deserted ruins, the stone jetty constructed without mortar, a pile of rotting creels, and westwards, open ocean to the new world, where so many from the island went in the time of the burning glens.

As she reaches the end of the track Marsaili notices a feature of the landscape she can't recollect from her visits here with her father, when they came for griddle scones and Gaelic conversation of the same light texture. There's a standing stone on the moor behind the houses which she's sure she hasn't seen before. This shows the fickleness of memory. She must be confusing it with another place. Marsaili notices something else. Smoke is rising from one of the buildings as she stops the Land Rover. A man emerges from the house and comes across to shake hands.

'I'm Fraser MacNab.'

He's a tall good-looking man, maybe in his late forties.

'I didn't think anyone lived here any more,' Marsaili tells him.

'I don't have a phone or a post-code.'

'Then how. . .'

'Did I get in touch with the surgery? I used the phone-box at the end of the road. That's where the postman leaves my mail. I told him, if it looks interesting, leave it on the shelf. If it's junk mail, don't waste your tyres. Tear it up.'

'You have a sick pony?' Marsaili enquired.

He led her round the house to a lean-to. A pony was lying on a heap of hay.

'She's beautiful,' Marsaili says. 'What is she?'

'An Eriskay.'

She remembers that one of her lecturers at vet school was fascinated by the breed.

'They're very rare,' the owner tells her. 'In fact they were thought to have died out, until a man in the Outer Isles revealed that he had a stallion. It took me a long time to get this mare. That's why I phoned.'

'What's wrong with her?' Marsaili asks, kneeling beside the pony.

'She stopped eating about three days ago.'

Marsaili hadn't examined a pony since her days on the island as George's apprentice. As she's feeling her stomach she's soothing her with her voice.

'I'm going to give her an injection,' she says, fetching her bag from the Land Rover.

'What's her name?' she asks as she inserts the needle.

'Raonaid.'

Marsaili is smiling in approval at the Gaelic name for Rachel.

'Would you like a cup of tea?' he asks.

She follows him into the house. She's sure it's the one that she used to visit with her father. The old range is still there, and the floor is flagstones. He lifts the globe from a lamp and turns up the lighted wick. The walls of slatted pine reflect the yellow glow of homeliness.

'How long have you been here?' she asks in wonder.

'About five years.'

'Do you belong to the island?' Marsaili enquires as she accepts the mug of tea and the rocking chair by the fire vacated by the cat. She remembers how the people of this house sat round the table, conversing in Gaelic with her father.

'The MacColl who owned this house was my uncle.'

'So you bought it?' Marsaili asked, intrigued.

'Why should I buy it? It was my people's house, run as a croft, and I assumed that since it was falling down, nobody was interested in it. So I started rebuilding it with my own hands.'

Marsaili liked this blond man's assertiveness as he stood by the fire, the cat in his arms.

'Did your father have Gaelic?' she asked.

'He didn't use it when he went to the city, and my mother

didn't have it, so I was deprived, though I didn't know it at the time. I'm learning it,' he told her, pointing to a pile of cassette tapes. 'It's difficult, but I'm getting there, now that I've got more time.'

'What do you do for a living?'

'I trained at the Glasgow School of Art and taught in a school in the city for maybe twelve years. It was a rough area by the river. The kids squeezed the paints out of the tubes, but it didn't land on the paper. In fact they set fire to my storeroom. I used to stand at the window with my eyes closed and think, I don't belong here; I belong to a peaceful place on the west coast I've never been to, but which I feel I've known all my life. So one day I walked out and came up here.'

'Just like that?' Marsaili said, impressed.

'I don't have a wife or family, and I had some money put aside, so it wasn't all that difficult. I came here to do two things – to find my roots and to work as an artist.'

Marsaili is looking round the walls for examples of his work.

'I don't believe in indoor art,' he's telling her. 'That's shutting the imagination out.'

She follows him in the gloaming past the lean-to where the Eriskay pony seems to be sleeping peacefully on her side.

'What am I to see?' she asks her companion.

'You said you came here a lot in the past. What's different?'

'I don't remember that stone,' she says, pointing to the pillar angled against the sky.

'That's because I put it there.'

'*You* put it there?'

He's talking as she's walking beside him.

'I found it lying on the moor and I brought it across here.'

'How did you manage that?' she asks in wonder as they approach the pillar of granite, taller than herself.

He has his hand on it now.

'I thought to myself, should I put the names of the MacColls on it as a monument, and then I thought, no, it's better to leave it blank, so that people can imprint it with their own imaginations.'

There were standing stones in other parts of the island, including a circle of three. But Marsaili was most impressed by this pillar standing on the moor, with the sea behind.

'No one knows why they put up these stones,' her companion is telling her as the cat winds round her legs.

'People used to say that they were sacrificial sites,' Marsaili recalls from her young days on the island, when old folk had told her father of feelings of terror they had had in the vicinity of the stones.

'I don't believe that. I think they were lunar calculators. You needed to know you were going to have enough moonlight for the harvest.'

'Is that why you put this stone up?' Marsaili asks.

A lapwing anxious about its nest is swooping at them as they go back towards the house.

'I'll come to see the pony tomorrow,' Marsaili tells him, holding out her hand. 'Thanks for the tea and the lesson on standing stones.'

Her mother is waiting at the window, convinced that there has been an accident. That's the legacy for having been married to a bad driver, a man who never sat a test. As a young man he used to roar round the roads on the mainland on a motor bike while she clasped his waist and later found blue heather bells in her shoes, the way he took the bends.

She doesn't tell her mother about the new man at the old township. She says she went for a walk because it's such a lovely evening, which isn't a lie. She drinks tea, sitting at the darkening window overlooking the bay. She's conscious tonight that she's an observer of her own past, as if that mast light out there belongs to the boat that she and Douglas have just brought into the bay, their young children asleep in their berths, her father still alive, waiting for her with his courtly manners and Gaelic stories. Here she is, a woman who must be near the menopause, and yet her heart has the lightness of the young girl she was, seeing a boy she fancied at the clock tonight. She isn't thinking of the stone on the moor; she's thinking of the Eriskay pony lying in the lean-to, with her sad eyes.

On this visit Marsaili wanted to have a serious talk with her mother about moving to the mainland. But she's not so sure now. Alice is probably better off here – despite her phobia about the weather – than in a city.

Marsaili was busy the next morning at the surgery and it was five o' clock before she could get away to see the pony.

'How is she?' she asked.

'Just the same,' the man says. 'I've made us supper.'

A lobster he's taken from one of his creels is bubbling in the pot, and there is a dish of potatoes with their skins still on which he dug up that afternoon from his patch by the sea.

The meal is delicious, she tells him.

'You made this?' she says when he puts the plate in front of her.

It's carraigean, of such lightness she hardly knows it's on the spoon.

'My mother used to buy it powdered in a shop in New City Road. Her people came from the north. I gathered the weed from the shore.'

He refuses her help with the washing-up and puts a coffee pot on the range. Then he plays one of his Gaelic tuition tapes. She says the phrase and he repeats it after her.

'You're getting the grasp of it,' she tells him. 'But what use will it be?'

'What do you mean?'

The phrase she has just uttered takes her too by surprise. She would never have said that in front of her father. When she was learning Gaelic, there were still people to speak it with. Now there can't be half a dozen people left in the town – and most of them over seventy – who have the language, and some of them are in Sunset Court with senile dementia, not even able to remember their own names, never mind stories in a language almost lost.

'There's nobody about here to speak it to.'

'That's not the point,' he says sharply. 'At least I'll have made the effort.'

She read somewhere – she has always been a great reader – that one theory of a haunted house is that somehow its history and voices have been etched on its walls, like a recording. These grooved pine walls around her must hold the Gaelic of generations singing about the sea, or telling stories about dead men being seen in boats. Maybe this man sitting opposite her, with his tuition tapes and his patience, his confidence in his own abilities, will tune into these walls as he sits here throughout the winter and emerge, a fluent speaker, out of his warm cocoon.

'I must go,' she says.

This man is becoming more attractive to her by the minute. If he offered her a bed here for the night, in the peace, she may not refuse.

'*Oidhche mhath*.'

He takes a torch and they go and check the pony. It still looks so poorly.

'You must think I'm not a very good vet.'

'I don't think that at all. It'll come round, you'll see.'

She was visiting him every evening now, telling her mother that she was going out to supper with friends. He would have the meal waiting for him. Tonight it's seafood pancakes, full of delicious flavours that recall her childhood, from the pail of crab claws, the silver fish left behind the storm door.

Afterwards they walked across the moor to the bed where he was taking his peats from, the same place used by his uncles.

'How do you get them back to the house?' she asked as she looked at the glistening black bank, the consistency of chocolate gateau.

'I could use the pony, but I carry the creel on my back, the way the uncles did.'

He was putting blocks from the pyramid into the creel, then hoisting it on to his back.

'It looks very heavy.'

'It's worth it, when you think of the light and warmth at the end.'

'You're a romantic.'

'I hope I am.'

She walked beside him, her hand out against the creel, as if she were helping to ease the burden. When they passed the wall she looked over at the pony.

'She doesn't seem to be getting any better. '

'She'll be fine,' he says. 'She's a hardy little beast.'

Marsaili likes sitting by the fire of fragrant peat he cut himself from the moor, giving him the pronunciation of Gaelic words and phrases. He's making progress and will soon be able to conduct a simple conversation. One evening he says, *mo ghoal.*

She looks up with surprise.

'You pronounced that well.'

'Because I mean it.'

My love. She flushed by the fire.

'We've got so much in common, Marsaili. We both love this island, we love Gaelic.'

She's about to unbutton her blouse in this room fragrant with the smoke from timber that covered this island maybe millions of years ago. Through the open door she can see his bed. She has waited long enough in homage to Douglas, maybe too long. It will be difficult returning to passion, because her body has got used to being alone, with no other hands touching it.

As she steps out of her skirt she looks out of the small back window, at the Eriskay pony lying in its enclosure, and the standing stone beyond it against the reddening sky. She has not seen this juxtaposition before, and the two things together bring to the surface of her mind the question that she didn't put, or that he didn't answer.

'How did you get the stone there?'

His bare back is to her. He's unbuckling the belt at his waist, about to ease down his denims.

'The pony pulled it.'

'From where?'

'Across the moor, about a quarter of a mile away,' he tells her without turning round.

'You made her pull a stone that size all that way?'

'We did it by stages.'

'Stages?'

'A few yards at a time.'

Then she sees the little mare, with the harness, striving to pull the pillar, against an ominous sky.

'You've strained her heart.'

'A few more days and she'll be fine,' he says, folding his denims now.

But she's stepping back into her skirt.

'You've damaged her heart,' she tells him angrily. 'She may have to be put down.'

'Leave it, Marsaili,' he advises her tersely, coming towards her naked.

But all her clothes are back on now.

'I won't leave it. I can't leave it. I'm a vet.'

He tries to put his arms around her but she pushes him away and goes outside. There is a breeze now coming from the darkening sea. Her mother may be right, there's bad weather out in the Atlantic. As she walks towards the lean-to she's thinking how her father too venerated the past. He loved his native language, the customs of the islands. But this was a society where women were bowed under the creel while their men drank and fought; a society where hands groped in the darkness when they didn't want that because it wasn't love, and anyway, they were exhausted.

Stones could be restored, but hearts couldn't. She goes into the lean-to and kneels beside the pony, lifting her head into her lap. She is hugging it and crying when the thunder breaks. She must get her mother off this awful island.

27.
Time to Go

Alice was watching television at home on the island when the picture suddenly went black and white. She phoned Fergie the engineer to report the fault, but when he came round later that evening he told her that there was no problem with the colour, and that she should see about her eyes.

Alice went to an optician on the mainland, who referred her to the hospital. The slim torch he shone into her eyes became a diminishing sun. She had macular degeneration, meaning that her central vision was going, and all the colour leaching out of the world.

How many shops had Marsaili and her mother trooped round, looking for vision aids? Alice acquired a large collection of magnifying glasses and illuminated lenses like torches. She also bought the kind of aid that embroiderers use for fine needlework, a square thick lens in a tortoiseshell frame, to be worn round the neck. Even then, Alice couldn't read the deaths column in the local paper, and Marsaili had to do it over the phone. When she suggested Talking Books, Alice got very angry. The blind people sent her a white-faced watch with large numerals, and a folding white cane which she put into the bin.

She had her stroke while visiting Marsaili in Glasgow. It happened about seven o' clock when her mother insisted on drying the supper dishes. Marsaili heard the plate spinning on the tiles, but by the time she got through her mother was holding on to the taps at the sink. The efficiency of the paramedics amazed Marsaili as they got the mask on her mother's ashen face. Marsaili went with her to the Infirmary and waited most of the night, because it was touch-and-go. When she was allowed to see Alice in the dawn, she was curled up in bed, like the photograph in the museum of the ancient body that had been dug out of a peat bog in the Ross on the island. Her mother had pneumonia, but she was tough and she had survived, though when the neurologist clipped the film of the scan to the light-box, Marsaili saw a brain cratered like the moon.

She couldn't go back to her house on the island, where she had lived alone for ten years, after the death of her husband, and Marsaili couldn't cope with her in Glasgow, because of her busy vet practice. A nursing home was the best solution, because she would get care and attention round the clock.

Time to go to Heaven,' Alice Maclean would call down to her daughter as the nurse strapped her into the invalid seat and pressed the button. Marsaili watched her mother being hoisted on the rail towards the big stained glass window on the landing, showing a ship in full sail on a blue sea of billows. The house in the west end of Glasgow had been built by a rich tobacco merchant, and one of his own ships had brought back the mahogany that had been used so extensively on the doors.

At first Alice had hated it, refusing to sit with the other residents in the lounge, and insisting on being taken through to the hall, where she sat alone in a wing armchair, very angry. As soon as she heard her daughter's footfall she would shout, 'Get me out of this awful place!'

Alice made the life of the staff hell. She got up during the night and appeared on the landing, shouting that she was going home on the next boat, except that the steamer she was thinking about – the *Lochspelvie* – had long since been lost at sea beyond the Hebrides. The doctor had to be called in, and he prescribed a pill to quieten her down. She sat silent and withdrawn in the hall, and at mealtimes, when they put the plastic apron around her, she wouldn't speak to the others at the table. Yet this was the woman who as the bank manager's wife on the island was always at social functions, sitting beside her husband in the Hebridean Hotel as he delivered the Immortal Memory.

Marsaili was in despair. She even considered taking early retirement and looking after her mother at home, but her GP warned her that she would be worn out within a year. So she endured the outbursts and the silences, sitting beside her mother's chair, holding her long thin hand. Alice was surrounded by a constant traffic of zimmers. The two-wheeled frames trundled past her, sometimes with handbags hanging from them, old people who suddenly stopped in the hall, wondering where they were going, because they had forgotten where their rooms were. They looked to the lady sitting in the wing armchair, her long elegant hand resting against her cheek, but she had no directions to offer them. The squeak of the wheels became the gangway being pulled away as the steamer was about to sail, taking with it one of her children back to the university.

They stood in the hall, leaning on their frames, and wet themselves out of frustration and fear. They had to be led away by the nurses and changed like children, but an hour later the same thing would happen. Marsaili had often wondered what the grinding sound was that came from a cupboard, until on one visit she saw a care assistant going in with a folded-up pad. They were being shredded. Trousers and skirts were cleaned on the premises, but you couldn't erase the stain of humiliation. The Irish woman who screamed like a minah bird said her rosary every night before being taken away in her wheelchair.

Marsaili specialised in domestic pets in her practice. Weeping men as well as women brought in their cats and dogs in their arms, and she had to tell them that the loved animal was too old, too worn out to save. 'It's better if we put it to sleep,' she would say, and allowed the owner to hold the paws while she administered the lethal injection.

So if there were euthanasia for animals, why not for people too? Marsaili wouldn't have argued this before her mother went into the nursing home, but the pathetic sights she had seen over the past year had convinced her that it was cruel and humiliating to keep the old alive.

There were times when Marsaili considered taking a drug from her surgery cupboard and rolling up the sleeve on her mother's frail arm in the hall of the Home, when no one was about. If it could put a sizeable dog to sleep, why not her mother too, without pain?

Marsaili has this image of her mother, the long fine hands folding up tombola tickets and dropping them into the drum in the sitting-room overlooking the bay. The tickets have been printed on the bank's inky Gestetner downstairs, and many of them say, *Sorry no luck*. Alice runs the tombola stall at the sale of work, spinning the drum and calling on people to have a go for sixpence, in the days of the old coinage. The lucky ones receive a miniature of whisky, home-baked gingerbread.

Alice was always so competent, born to be a mother. From the day of her marriage she had dedicated herself to her husband and then to the four children who arrived over a span of ten years. She buckled them into their little kilts and took them to Sunday school.

She closed the curtains when they had measles, in case they damaged their eyes. She sat commiserating with them when they had fallen out with their first loves, and when they brought partners home from university she was most welcoming, helping the drunken Calum up to his bed during his prolonged bender following his anguish over Iona McPhee's baby. Alice carefully steamed the salmon that was left behind the storm door of the house, as a gift to the bank manager who did the fishermen's tax.

Alice was busy from morning till night, changing beds, turning the tombola wheel, sitting in the audience watching her husband compere the weekly ceilidh for the summer visitors.

Marsaili continued to put down adored pets, sending heartbroken old women home without their companions. A child who brought in a golden hamster in cupped hands had to be told that it had cancer, and that sleep was the kindest course. But it wasn't all bad news. The black labrador left the surgery with a white ruff round its neck, so that it wouldn't touch the wound it had got on the flank from barbed wire. A lizard escaped its box and took an hour to capture, with much laughter.

After another seizure Alice developed dementia. She would chant '*Lochspelvie! Lochspelvie!*' as if she were facing another voyage down the sound on a dark stormy night. Some evenings when Marsaili went in her mother complained about the gale, though it was still evening outside.

Then, as the dementia deepened, Alice became calmer. The winds abated in her mind. She was a young woman again, sailing up the blue sound on the *Lochspelvie*, her children on the slatted seat beside her. Trudie the terrier, long since buried beside Gille Ruadh's Dìleas, was at Alice's heels again as she walked along Main Street with her basket, greeting the dead. Her own mother, twenty years gone, came to visit at the Glasgow nursing home, and her late husband was a constant presence. Uncles, aunts, nephews were all welcomed. Marsaili couldn't deny the existence of these ghosts, otherwise her mother became very upset, crying that she was 'going mad'.

Marsaili realised that the roles were being reversed. She was the one who was getting older. Alice was reverting to infancy, having to be fed cut-up food by her daughter, supping her tea from a plastic nipple.

In the following months, Alice was to die several times. Marsaili would be summoned from her bed in the dawn by a call from the Home, telling her that her mother's breathing had changed. She sat holding Alice's hand, waiting for the minute, but she rallied and by evening she would be sitting up, eating her supper. The Matron said that she was a strong woman, and Marsaili began to realise that she had been even stronger than her husband, who seemed to have inexhaustible energy, inexhaustible fun.

Alice had gone back, through her children's childhood, into her own childhood, talking the incomprehensible language of the nursery, and now curled up in the foetal position. The woman who had feared the sea so much was drowning in her own lungs, until calm morning came.

On a summer evening Marsaili went back to the island, to clear the house for sale. Blinded by tears, she slipped the watch into an envelope, to send it back to the Institute for the Blind, together with a donation. The late banker had clattered out his ceilidh and after-dinner verses and addresses on the typewriter in his office, and after they were delivered to standing ovations Alice had stuffed the texts into a drawer which Marsaili had to force open. Who could deliver them like Archie Maclean?

There was so much accumulated stuff of such good quality that Marsaili couldn't send it to the dump, so she put a notice in Black's, inviting people to come up the stairs and help themselves. But nobody wanted the sagging bed, and Marsaili herself undid the bolts with a spanner and carried the awkward irons down the turnpike stairs, holding them aloft like lances, as though she were going to a tournament in the time of the Celtic heroes. The mattress on which she had been conceived and on which the Gaelic scholar had lain went to the dump. Later that afternoon, when she went out on to Main Street, there was nobody to converse with in Gaelic.

Other Books
from Argyll Publishing

The Machine Doctor
Peter Burnett
Thirsty Books ISBN:1 902831 33 0 pbk £9.99

". . . an exhilarating and anarchic comedy shot through with a
withering social commentary. " **Scotland on Sunday**

". . . an ambitious, multi-voiced satire on the soul-destroying
mind-numbing effects of the 21st century. . . hilarious"
The List

". . . ingenious . . . it has energy and commitment, it is funny
and makes a serious point lightly" **The Herald**

The Wind in her Hands
Margaret Gillies Brown
ISBN:1 902831 41 1 pbk £7.99

'an intruging picture of life early last century' **Caledonia**

'it never flags – the story of a strong woman' **Moray Firth Radio**

'inspirational' **Press & Journal**

Available in bookshops or direct from Argyll Publishing,
Glendaruel, Argyll PA22 3AE Scotland
For credit card, full stock list and other enquiries
tel 01369 820229 argyll.publishing@virgin.net
or visit our website www.skoobe.biz